THE SCHRÖDINGER ENIGMA

GREG KROJAC

GREG KROJAC

This book or any portion thereof may not be reproduced or used in any manner whatsoever without the express permission of the author except for the use of brief quotations in a book review.

Please note that this book is a work of fiction and any resemblance to persons, living or dead, or places, events or locales is purely coincidental. The characters are productions of the author's imagination and used fictitiously.

Copyright © 2018 Greg Krojac
All rights reserved

Language:UK English

PAPERBACK EDITION

GREG KROJAC

DEDICATION

Dedicated to Eliene for her patience and understanding while I hide myself away and write.

Schrödinger's Cat

Schrödinger's Cat is a thought experiment about quantum physics, suggested by Erwin Schrödinger in 1935, which says that if you were to place a cat and something that could kill the cat (a radioactive atom) in a box and seal it, you would not know if the cat was dead or alive until you opened the box; until the box was opened, the cat would be (in a sense) in two simultaneous states - both "dead and alive".

GREG KROJAC

DAY ONE – 24 APRIL

The crew of the F/V Alaskan Mermaid was looking forward to a well-earned rest from the arduous work of trawling in the icy waters of the Bering Sea. The Pollock A season was almost officially over and, like most of the other factory trawlers, the Alaskan Mermaid would normally have returned home before the season's end, allowing the crew to take a welcome early break and spend quality time with their families. But destiny had played a cruel card and forced the freezer trawler to stay out at sea when it suffered a major failure in the factory freezer equipment; its refrigerant was partially released into the engine room. A similar thing had happened to another trawler the previous season, but with far more calamitous consequences - the stricken trawler had developed a list due to an accumulation of seawater on the starboard side, the ship was abandoned, and less than half an hour later, the ship had down-flooded and slipped beneath the waves, stern first.

Valuable lessons had been learned from that incident and the inquest's recommendations rapidly put in place, allowing prompt action by the crew of the Alaskan Mermaid to minimize the damage, and avoid the same fate. The result was only a few days loss of fishing while essential repairs were made.

Now the ship was up and running again and scores of seabirds swarmed above the cold waters, each one peering downward with beady eyes, ready to pounce upon any gift that the sea was forced to give up. Suddenly the icy water erupted and the birds became even more agitated. The water swelled around the centre of the disturbance as a net broached its surface, a heaving mass of fish pushing against the nylon netting from within, as the catch gradually made its way towards the stern of the fishing boat. After a couple of minutes, the rest of the net surfaced, an industrial strength fishnet stocking, the foot section crammed with aquatic booty, as the heavy-duty winch hauled the trawl closer and closer to the waiting crewmen, A few birds pecked at the extremities of fish that poked out between the netting, but most of the gulls had dispersed and were taking advantage of other fish that had been brought to the surface by the turbulence.

This was a good catch, the trawl filled to bursting point with thousands of squirming rusty pink fish. As it got ever closer to the trawler, the net flattened out and some of the fish made a break for freedom. But there was nowhere safe to swim to, and the fleeing fugitives were easily picked off by the aerial scavengers. For those trapped within the trawler net, their fate was sealed and they would surely end up on somebody's dinner table. As the sea surrendered its grip on the teeming treasure, the netting began to accelerate towards its destination.

The pulley creaked a little under the weight of the day's haul, as the struggle to reel in the day's catch began in earnest. The ship's captain stood on the bridge, watching the booty as it glistened in the morning sun, pleased with what he saw. They would soon be able to head back to port and see their families again – that's what kept them all going. Trawling for Pollock was a hard life and everybody on board was eager for respite from the arduous work. Suddenly the trawler's skipper spotted something unusual in the nets, something that had no business being there. He leaned into his microphone and bellowed an order which resounded around the ship.

"Stop the winch!"

The crew couldn't see why the command had been given, but they knew that he must have a good reason. The winch stopped abruptly, complaining briefly at the unexpected interruption. The captain barked another order.

"Cut engines."

The ship became silent, or at least as silent as is possible for a working factory ship. The deck crew, now with nothing to do for the moment, crowded at the stern of the ship, staring at the now stilled net, the fish within still thrashing about trying to escape. The captain ordered the ship's engines to restart, and the vessel to edge forward as slowly as possible, so that the trawl net wouldn't sink back underwater. He passed his binoculars to his first mate, who had been standing alongside him all the time.

"Take a look, Robert, and tell me what you see."

Robert put the binoculars to his eyes and changed the focus so that he could see better what had caused the net retrieval to be paused.

"It looks like a satellite dish, Skip, but surely it's too big for that. And what the hell would a satellite dish be doing out here in the middle of the Bering Sea?"

"Take another look, Robert."

The first mate refocused the binoculars.

"No, it's not a satellite dish. I think it may actually be a satellite."

The captain had been mulling silently through his options while watching the object bob up and down in the water.

"Agreed. But if it is a satellite, whose is it? It may be one of ours. maybe not. But we definitely can't deal with it ourselves. As much as I'd love to claim it as salvage, the authorities will want to know what we've found. But – on the bright side – I wouldn't be surprised if there's a finder's fee. I'll get on the satphone to the Coastguard. They'll know what to do."

Robert grinned.

"Let's hope it's not the satellite we need to make that call."

The call was made and then the two of them descended the steps from the bridge to the ship's deck. Robert called over two of the crewmen.

"Fancy a swim?"

The two men certainly did. Normally their task was to make underwater repairs or release a snagged trawl and it would be good to do something different. It wasn't every day that a satellite got caught in a trawler's nets, and they wanted to get a better look at the day's celebrity.

Five minutes later, all kitted up in their scuba-diving gear, they plunged into the water and headed to the part of the net where the object was trapped. Each had with them a length of rope which they used to further constrain the object in case the sea had any thoughts of dragging it back down below. Then they checked the area around the satellite and dived underwater to see what was happening beneath the netting. A few seconds later they resurfaced and gave a thumbs up to the captain, who looked visibly relieved. The satellite – and the windfall that it hopefully represented – wasn't going anywhere.

"Robert, tell the divers to attach a buoy to it and then come back on board. We can't afford to lose it."

An hour or so later, the chud-chud-chud of helicopter blades could be heard in the distance. The sound got louder as the chopper continued to approach the ship until it was close enough to drop three divers into the water near the net. Now the entire crew was on deck watching the adventure unfold, and at least two dozen cell-phones were pointed at the scene, recording the event for both posterity and social media.

Sitara Khan had been given no chance to prepare for this trip. No sooner had she received the phone call, than a car had pulled up outside her aunt's house in Anchorage, ready to whisk her away to a waiting helicopter at the nearby Joint Base Elmendorf-Richardson. She'd been enjoying her break from her work as a member of the Voyager Team at the Jet Propulsion Labs at Caltech, but the Deputy Administrator of NASA – actually his PA – had called her personally, so she could hardly refuse. She grabbed a few clothes, stuffed them into a backpack, and called out to her aunt.

"I have to go out for a while. Don't worry if I'm not back tonight – I have to do something for work – I expect I'll be back tomorrow."

Her aunt didn't worry too much. She knew her niece was a sensible girl, with an important job. Sitara wasn't a typical Muslim woman; a child of the 90s, she had missed the Islamic dictatorship back in Pakistan. This had allowed her certain freedoms of thought and choice, and she'd been able to follow her dream of a career in science. She'd been inspired by the example of Muslim astronaut Anousheh Ansari, who had spent time on the International Space Station back in 2006. Science wasn't necessarily the career path that her family would have chosen for her – they'd have loved for her to be a doctor or lawyer - but Sitara had been adamant that she wanted to break the stereotype and work for NASA. Her parents had given her their blessing and sent her to study at MIT in Cambridge, Massachusetts, where she had graduated. At any other university, she would have probably graduated *Cum Laude*, but she had set her heart on MIT. And, unlike some of her friends, this wasn't a ruse to escape being married off. Sitara had a dream which her family had allowed her to follow. They were very proud of their daughter.

Sitara knew that something big was going on as soon as she was ushered towards a US Navy helicopter. She climbed aboard and then watched the Alaskan coast fade into the distance behind her. She was part of the Mission Control team, whose job was to send instructions to and receive data from a space probe that was 13 billion miles from Earth in interstellar space and moving further away at a rate of 1 million miles a day. It was pure chance that, on that particular day, she was the closest available NASA/JPL, and so the task of representing NASA on site fell to her. She'd taken a scuba-diving course on her days off from the Pasadena based JPL offices back in California, and that skill was about to pay dividends.

Soon she was plunging into the icy waters of the Bering Sea, flanked by two Navy frogmen whose primary duty was to keep her safe. One of the frogmen cut away a portion of the netting, just enough to provide easier access to the object and dozens of fish, suddenly seeing an opportunity for freedom, poured out of their nylon cage. Sitara was thankful for her wetsuit – she didn't mind swimming with fish around her but didn't much like the idea of scores of fleeing fish battering her naked skin.

Once she got closer to it, she scanned the surface of the tethered object, looking for anything that could help identify it. If Sitara didn't know better she'd have said that she was looking at a space probe, but that was patently ridiculous, so she pushed such thoughts to the back of her mind. Obviously, it had to be a satellite – she just needed to discover its country of origin.

Looking over the dish part of the object, she could see what appeared to be a High Gain Antenna along with a Subreflector Support Truss and Subreflector, but logic told her that the suspicions that were seeping into her mind had to be wrong and she tossed them away. She dipped underwater and her waterproof flashlight lit up a ten-sided box with container bays attached to the base of what she believed to be an antenna. She opened one of the bays, expecting to see radio transmitters or various electronic subsystems and scientific instruments, but was shocked to find that it was empty. She hurriedly opened the other nine compartments, only to find that they too were empty. It didn't make sense; nobody would send a satellite into orbit without at least some technical purpose.

She noticed that there were a number of mountings on the craft with nothing attached to them. She wracked her brains, trying to think what might be missing from those supports, and then it hit her like a thunderbolt out of the blue. She'd seen the configuration before, not first-hand admittedly, but she had read enough technical documents and seen enough photos and illustrations that she should have followed her initial and absurd gut feelings. She was so busy trying to prove to herself that the object was a fallen satellite, certain in the knowledge that the alternative couldn't possibly be true, that she had momentarily abandoned her scientific impartiality. But the alternative was ludicrous and she'd felt justified in dismissing it. She had never expected to see the object with her own eyes – it had left Earth over forty years earlier on a one-way journey into space. It was most definitely not supposed to be back on its home planet.

There should have been an arm at the end of which were located a Low-Energy Charged Particle Detector, a Cosmic Ray Subsystem, a Plasma Subsystem, an Imaging Science Subsystem, an Ultraviolet Spectrometer, the Photopolarimeter Subsystem, and an Infrared Interferometer Spectrometer. Was she losing her mind? The spacecraft was billions of miles away. She looked again. Something else had been connected to the unit, but it hadn't broken off – it had been deliberately removed. She moved to the other side of the container housing, what she now knew had to be the Bus. Other items had also been carefully removed. She knew what should have been there – an Optical Calibration Target plate, two Planetary Radio Astronomy and Plasma Wave Antennae, three Radioisotope Thermoelectric Generators, and a

Magnetometer Boom. She knew exactly what the object was, except that it couldn't be. Her bosses would think her insane. She looked again at the main body of the Bus, desperately seeking anything that could convince her otherwise. Another missing item was conspicuous by its absence. The plinth was there but it was no longer attached to anything. And what should have been there would have confirmed beyond all reasonable doubt the identity of the object. The Golden Record was missing. A chill ran down her spine as she realized the magnitude of what the sea had just given up. How was she going to explain to NASA that one of its Voyager space probes had come home?

DAY TWO – 25 APRIL

Infected 60 Dead 0

The NASA conference room in Washington DC looked like many a conference room up and down the country; a horseshoe of linked desks, the open end of the arrangement providing easy visibility to two wafer-thin large-screen TV monitors hanging on a wall, a giant one complemented by a smaller one placed centrally beneath it. To each side of the smaller TV was a framed picture of each Voyager space probe, Voyager One to the left and Voyager Two to the right, each probe encircled by images of the prime members of its project team. Each individual desk was furnished with its own computer monitor and almost all the blue executive office chairs were occupied. The people seated were of all shapes, sizes, and ethnicities, some in their late twenties and others up to thirty years or so older than their colleagues. Most of the eighteen were male, although six were women and, with the entrance of Dr Sitara Khan, that number was now increased to seven. Sitara had the typical extreme beauty and lighter complexion of her Pathan heritage, coupled with large dark eyes that looked as if they had been drawn by a Disney artist. The majority of the men were dressed formally in shirt and tie, but a handful – the younger ones mainly – were wearing polo-shirts. All present had NASA identity cards hanging from blue cords slung around their necks.

Sitara mouthed hello to several of the attendees as she made her way to a vacant chair in front of the main monitors and upon whose desk sat a nameplate with the word 'PRESENTER' etched in silver capital letters on a black background. She wasn't the most important person at the meeting by rank – that would be Anthony Healey, the Administrator of NASA – but, as the NASA representative at the scene of the salvage, her input would be the most valuable. The task of chairing the meeting fell to the NASA Deputy Administrator who, along with the Administrator, and the respective Directors of JPL, the Goddard Space Flight Center (GSFC), the Langley Research Center (LRC), and the Independent Verification and Validation Facility (IVVF), was anxious to hear what Sitara had to say.

Sitara settled into her seat, and smiled at the three other members of the Voyager One Project Team at the meeting; the Project Manager, the Voyager Spacecraft Team Chief, and the Telecommunications and Mission Systems Manager, She didn't normally occupy such a high profile position in meetings, but this time she held a unique position in the chain of evidence. She was a nervous, a little in awe of being in the presence of so many high-ranking NASA officials at the same time, but did her best to conceal it. The Deputy Administrator rose to his feet, adjusted his suit jacket, cleared his throat and began to speak.

"Ladies and gentlemen, thank you for coming here at such short notice. However, when you hear what Dr Khan has to say, I'm sure that you will agree that it was well worth the inconvenience. So, without further ado, I would like to hand you over to Voyager Project Scientist, Dr Sitara Khan."

The Deputy Administrator retook his seat as Sitara stood up. She had given presentations dozens of times since she'd joined the agency, but this particular presentation had been very hastily prepared. However, everybody in the room knew this and wouldn't be judging her on the slickness of her performance. Sitara pressed a key on her notebook computer and the larger of the screens displayed a website entitled 'Voyager, The Interstellar Mission'. To calm her nerves, she took a sip from the glass of water that had been provided for her. Her throat freshly moistened, she felt more confident.

"Good morning Administrator, and good morning Deputy Administrator, ladies and gentlemen. What I am going to say will seem impossible but I ask you all to keep an open mind."

Everybody nodded silently. Sitara continued.

"May I first draw your attention to the main screen? You'll see three measurements for each of the two Voyager spacecraft. Please notice, in particular, the distance of the Voyager 1 space probe from Earth.

It's shown in both kilometres and AUs, with its distance from the Sun, and the roundtrip light time from the Earth. It's nothing unusual. We've all seen these figures and watched them as they increase by the second. We've seen them hundreds of times. Thousands. But I want you to be aware of them while you listen to what I have to say.

"Twenty-four hours ago I was up to my neck in the waters of the Bering Sea, behind a fishing trawler, examining an object that had been caught in their nets. I'd been visiting my aunt in Anchorage when I received an urgent phone call from NASA to drop everything and go investigate an unidentified object. I fully expected it to be sunken space debris or perhaps, at best, a fallen satellite."

Another key press and the advancing distances were replaced by a photo of the object trapped within the trawler's netting, the website now displayed on the smaller screen. This photo then dissolved to reveal another image of the object, this time sitting captive in a JPL laboratory at Pasadena. Her audience murmured as Sitara took a deep breath, knowing that she was about to say the unthinkable, that she was about to say what they were all thinking.

"The spacecraft that we recovered from the sea is Voyager One."

A hush fell over the room. The assembled scientists knew what the object looked like, but Sitara had said the unutterable. She studied the confused faces that now mirrored her own at the moment when she'd come to the same conclusion.

"I had my suspicions as soon as I saw the object, but they were confirmed when I began to examine the Bus at the base of the High Gain Antenna. I noticed that there were other mountings with nothing attached to them. That's when alarm bells really started ringing. I opened each of the ten compartments, in turn, expecting to find electronic subsystems and instrumentation – but they were empty. They were all empty."

Administrator Healey interrupted Sitara. The very thought that the vehicle in their labs being examined by their scientists could be Voyager One was irrational, but the empty compartments of whatever the spacecraft was concerned him too.

"Doctor Khan, are you saying that these compartments had been opened, the contents deliberately removed, and then resealed?"

The Administrator listened to the words as he said them, thinking how preposterous they sounded when spoken out loud. Whatever it was, the object couldn't be Voyager One.

"They certainly appear to have been, yes."

"Could they not have been damaged by collision with a foreign object wandering the Solar System?"

"Perhaps, sir. But there's no evidence of any impact – other than expected pitting, that is. The Bus is intact. The compartments do seem to have been opened and resealed."

"Could they have been interfered with here on Earth? Before we recovered the object?"

"Of course there's always a small chance that

they were, but I don't believe that happened. Why would anyone remove some parts and leave the others? Surely it would make more sense to take the whole spacecraft."

Sitara knew how crazy she sounded. Voyager One was over thirteen billion miles away. Another murmur flowed around the room, as the audience tried to process what they had just heard. The objective of the two Voyager missions was to explore the Solar System and then to seek out new horizons and possibly encounter new civilizations. Nobody wanted to say the words but everybody understood the implications of the missing parts having been removed, and not broken off. Sitara waited for the hubbub to die down.

"I suspected that I was looking at Voyager One, but didn't want to believe it myself. I mean, it's crazy. Isn't it? But several other pieces of equipment were clearly missing, among them several Subsystems, Spectrometers, Antennae, and Thermoelectric Generators. None had been broken off; they had all been dismounted."

The audience watched as photos of the mountings to the supports upon which the equipment had been mounted zoomed into view. The removal had definitely been deliberate. The Administrator stood up.

"This is impossible. It can't be Voyager One. It must be a copy, although I can't for the life of me think why anyone would want to dump a fake space probe into the ocean."

He turned and pointed to the smaller screen, which was still showing the two Voyagers' distances from the Earth. The values were still increasing.

"Look. There's the proof. Both Voyagers are still there, travelling away from us. Voyager One can't be in two places at the same time. It's impossible. This has to be some kind of hoax. What other explanation could there possibly be?"

The Director of the IVVF offered a possible explanation.

"Perhaps we've unknowingly suffered a cyber-attack, perhaps our network's been hacked. Perhaps those numbers changing on the screen are false."

The Administrator shook his head.

"No, it can't be as simple as that. Firstly, we have one of the most robust IT security systems in the world. I hesitate to say we're 100 percent safe but we're as close as it's possible to get without calling ourselves perfect. And – even if that scenario were true – it would mean that Voyager One has turned around and returned to Earth in a matter of a few days. Considering that it's been travelling in the other direction for over forty years, I think we can rule that one out, don't you?"

The Deputy Administrator interjected.

"It's madness, I know. But our top forensic scientists have been examining the object non-stop since it arrived at the lab, and all the evidence is pointing to the object indeed being Voyager One. The same space probe that was launched from Cape Canaveral on September 5, 1977."

The Administrator shook his head.

"Which it can't be. The laws of physics don't allow for it. This has to be a hoax."

The Administrator pointed again to the ever-increasing distances displayed on the lower screen.

"I mean. Look. It's out there. Systems have been checked, double-checked, triple-checked. Voyager One has left our Solar System and is getting further and further away from us. That's Voyager One out there - what we have in our lab simply cannot be Voyager One."

Sitara was tempted to bite her lip, but she had to say something.

"Unless…"

The Administrator was prepared to hear any suggestion at the moment.

"Unless what, Dr Khan? I'm open to any suggestions."

"It sounds crazy."

"Spit it out, Doctor. We're looking crazy square in the eyes already. You can't make it any worse."

"Well, a few minutes earlier, you said that Voyager One can't be in two places at the same time."

"It can't."

"But what if it can? I mean, I know how it sounds, but perhaps it is in two places at the same time? We've proved that an electron can be in two places at one time. So can photons. What if it's only because we don't yet have the technology to do so that we can't do the same with larger objects? What if extra-terrestrials have developed advanced technology to do so? It sounds impossible, yes, but if we weren't open to the possibility of there being intelligent life being out there in the cosmos, SETI wouldn't exist. And we certainly wouldn't have put the Golden Records on the two Voyagers. Those compartments didn't open, remove the contents, and then close by themselves. And the missing equipment didn't just fall off. It was taken. As Arthur Conan Doyle wrote – once you eliminate the impossible, whatever remains, no matter how improbable, that must be considered the truth."

Sitara had the bit between her teeth. Normally she wouldn't have had the nerve to propose such an outlandish hypothesis. The whole situation was unprecedented; perhaps an absurd suggestion wouldn't necessarily be out of place.

"It's like Schrödinger's Cat. Voyager One is here on Earth, being examined by our forensic team, while simultaneously being over thirteen billion miles away travelling out of the Solar System. With no definitive evidence to the contrary, until we can prove otherwise, we have to accept that somehow Voyager One is both here and out there in Space. Voyager One is Schrödinger's Cat."

Ever since Voyager One had left Earth in 1977, it had been communicating with the home planet and was still doing so. The signal would eventually be irretrievable, but that hadn't happened yet. It had sent back data about Saturn, Jupiter, and Jupiter's moon Titan, information that could only have been obtained if the space probe were physically in those locations. The Deep Space Network of antenna arrays had continued to send and receive messages even though the spacecraft was now at least in the heliosphere if not travelling outside the Solar System. Admittedly, having access to the Deep Space Network for only six to eight hours per day, it was entirely possible that Voyager scientists wouldn't actually be physically monitoring the craft if something extraordinary were to happen, but nothing untoward had occurred as far as they were aware – certainly nothing like a return to Earth at technologically impossible speeds.

Then there was the fact that equipment had been removed from the earthbound space probe. That would infer both intelligence and dexterity, meaning that the probe had succeeded in making contact with extra-terrestrial beings; a fascinating yet simultaneously frightening thought. Not wishing to look foolish, the common consensus at the meeting concurred with the Administrator. The spacecraft at JPL had to be a fake.

DAY THREE – 26 APRIL

Infected 281 Dead 0

"What do you mean, he's not saying anything? Didn't he come forward of his own accord?"

Sitting at his desk in his spacious Washington office, the Administrator had a good idea what the response to his question would be. If he were in the same position he too would insist on some reward. The Deputy Administrator outlined the retiree's demands.

"He wants immunity from prosecution and his pension upgraded to a full senior management pension with a lump sum payment of two hundred and fifty thousand dollars."

Administrator Tony Healey shook his head.

"He's asking a lot."

"He knows that, but he also realises the enormity of the situation at hand. He has a granddaughter with severe medical problems and says he needs to safeguard her future."

"But how does he know about our Voyager One conundrum?"

Deputy Administrator Roger Nelson paused for a second. He didn't like to admit the obvious answer.

"I don't know. I guess we have a leak somewhere."

"Shit."

"Shit indeed, Tony. We need to find out who it is, but that'll have to wait for the moment."

"Agreed. Put another hundred thousand dollars in the pot, but don't use it unless we have to."

"Understood."

The Administrator stood up and paced around the room for a few seconds, his right hand stroking his neatly coiffured beard. He placed both hands palm-down on top of his large mahogany desk and leaned into them.

"And make it conditional on his agreement to a polygraph. I know he has us by the balls, and that lie-detector tests aren't how we would normally do things, but he doesn't know that. I need time to get the President on board. Pardons are his department This man may have committed treason."

Three hours later, ex-assembly engineer Jonas Wade was sitting in a sparsely furnished and dimly lit room, facing an emotionless heavy-set man whose receding dark hair was just beginning to grey at the temples. On the table that separated them was a polygraph machine. Jonas Wade didn't much like the idea of having to undergo this procedure, but he needed the money. The emotionless man's assistant attached nodes onto various parts of Jonas's body and nodded to the interrogator, who looked straight into the eyes of the engineer.

"Good morning, Mr Wade. My name is Mr Anderson. I shall ask you a number of questions which I want you to answer truthfully. The first few questions will be to provide a benchmark in order to analyse your responses. Do you understand?"

Jonas nodded his agreement and Mr Anderson started his interrogation, while the Administrator and his deputy looked on from the other side of a two-way mirror.

"What is your job, Mr Wade?"

"I'm retired. Before that, I was an assembly engineer for JPL."

"Were you involved in the assembly of the Voyager One space probe, Mr Wade?"

"Yes sir, I was."

The needle of the polygraph machine busily darted up and down the paper. So far none of the responses was unexpected. After several more simple questions, Mr Anderson moved on to a more relevant line of questioning.

"You say that you can provide proof that the space probe in our custody, is the very same spacecraft which you helped assemble. Is that true?"

Jonas took a deep breath. He knew that he needed to be honest if he were to receive his payment. He wasn't dealing with fools.

"I believe so."

Outside the room, the Administrator turned to his Deputy.

"I believe so?"

The interrogator turned his head towards the reflective glass and nodded. The Deputy Administrator clarified the response.

"Technically, it means that he does believe that he can prove whether our space probe is the real Voyager One or not. It's as good as a yes – in these circumstances."

"So, as far as he is concerned, what he is going to tell us is the truth?"

"Exactly."

Mr Anderson showed no emotion but inside he was secretly excited. The information that he was about to become privy to was extraordinary. He would love to have been able to tell his wife about his day when he got home that night, but he knew he couldn't. He'd be professional. He turned back to face Jonas.

"What is this proof, Mr Wade?"

Jonas knew that he was about to cross a line, that he would be unable to retract what he was about to confess, but his daughter needed certain house conversions to be made in order to make his disabled granddaughter's life more comfortable. He knew what he was doing.

"May I have a cigarette?"

The interrogator's assistant pointed to a no smoking sign on the wall. Jonas shrugged his shoulders.

"No harm in asking."

The interrogation continued.

"How can you prove that the space probe we have in custody is the original Voyager One?"

Jonas grinned. Not a sardonic grin but more a grin of self-indulgent pleasure as he remembered what he had done on that day over forty years ago.

"I left some of my DNA on the inside of one of them there panels. Just a small speck of blood, you know, but still enough for part of me to go into space."

The Administrator and the Deputy looked at each other aghast. Did he really just say that? Surprised as Mr Anderson was at this revelation, he didn't react and simply continued his line of questioning.

"How did you do that?"

"I was responsible for mounting the communication subsystem into one of the Bus compartments. It was a simple thing to nick my finger and leave a tiny bloodstain on a mounting bracket before attaching the subsystem to the back of the compartment. Especially back then."

"What do you mean, especially back then?"

"Well, security is surely much better now. I'm sure I couldn't do it these days without being spotted."

"Tell us how you did it."

Jonas's confidence was growing.

"There's no point in telling you now. It was forty plus years ago. Systems and processes have completely changed. I did it. That's all you need to know."

The interrogator changed the direction of the questioning.

"Why did you do it?"

"Call me an old fool if you like, but I'd always wanted to be an astronaut. I also knew that it was never going to happen. I was never fit enough, not even back then when I was younger. So I thought I'd do the next best thing and send a bit of me into space."

Administrator Healey wanted to know how his staff hadn't spotted the bloodspot during their forensic investigations, but that would have to wait. He took his phone from his pocket and sent a text to the investigating team supervisor to stop what they were doing and remove the panels from the communications subsystem compartment for more intensive screening.

The interrogator felt his phone vibrate in his pocket and took it out, tapping the touchscreen to activate the display. He read the message silently and then repeated its content.

"We'll need a sample of your DNA, Mr Wade. Do you agree to us taking a saliva sample?"

Jonas felt that now he was in control of the situation.

"It'll cost you another fifty thousand bucks."

The interrogator's phone vibrated again.

"Agreed."

Jonas was happy with that.

"Fifty grand, just for spitting into a test-tube. That's what I call a bargain."

Administrator Healey returned to his office with his deputy, leaving Mr Anderson to identify the source of the leak, and poured a couple of large scotches for himself and his deputy. He sat down in a burgundy leather armchair, his favourite of the two that were in his office, and rested his glass on the coffee table that separated the two men. Roger Nelson, sitting opposite him in a matching chair, took a sip of his own drink and placed it back on the table. Tony Healey leaned forward a little.

"So Roger. What do you think? Do you think that this may be the proof we're looking for?"

The Deputy nodded.

"It looks like it, Tony. It all depends if the DNA's survived the rigours of space. There was a recent experiment that proved that genetic material could survive a flight through space and re-entry into Earth's atmosphere, at least for a short journey. It was proven by a team of scientists from the University of Zurich. But we have no idea if DNA could have survived for this long and over such a large distance. But – and it's a 'but' with a capital B - if there's enough of it still intact, and it matches that of Jonas Wade, a whole new can of worms will open up."

The Administrator took his first sip of whisky.

"I don't know what I fear most, Roger. That the probe here is an elaborate hoax, or that it *is* the same probe we launched forty years ago. If the DNA matches, it'll raise so many questions like how did it get here? Why is it here? What does that mean for the

Voyager we're still getting signals from, the one that's over thirteen billion miles away? Is that a phantom? Is our equipment faulty? And what about Voyager Two for that matter?"

The Deputy needed another sip of whisky.

"Or, even scarier, what if they're both the real Voyager One like Doctor Khan suggested? That would suggest technology that defies the laws of physics as we understand them. And, if that's the case, what the hell do whoever the hell they are want?"

At a maximum security JPL laboratory in Pasadena, a small group of men and women were gazing through a toughened glass window at a physically impossible sight, the Voyager One space probe. As Voyager One had returned to Earth from deep space it had been automatically designated a Restricted Class V contamination risk, in line with the "Outer Space" Treaty of 1967. The group was dressed in full biological insulation protective garments and had undergone a rigorous decontamination process, just as the spacecraft had done before the JPL technical staff began their analyses and investigations. The fear of cross-contamination in either direction was very real, and nobody – not even the President of the United States – was exempt from the process.

The President had, understandably, been kept informed of the recent return to Earth of the space probe and had been advised not to visit the laboratory where it was being examined, but, being the type of person he was, he'd ignored the advice of his advisors and insisted on making the trip to JPL to see the celebrity spaceship (as he liked to call it) for himself. He pointed to the object on the other side of the glass.

"I want to go in there and see the spaceship close up."

Gerald Rickman, the Director of JPL, shook his head.

"I'm sorry Mr President, but I'm afraid you can't go in there."

The President gave the Director a steely stare.

"I'll pretend I didn't hear that, Gerald. I assume all decontamination protocols have been followed to the letter?"

"Well, yes Mr President. Of course. But that doesn't mean – "

"Doesn't mean what, Gerald?"

"It doesn't mean that it's completely one hundred percent safe."

The President gestured to the half a dozen technicians on the other side of the glass who were working on the space probe.

"If it's not safe, then why are they in there?"

The Director was becoming flustered. How do you say no to this particular President of the United States and keep your job? Men in higher positions than him had been dismissed from their posts, for far lesser reasons.

"But you're the President. You're the most important man in this great nation. You're the leader of the free world. We can't risk anything happening to you."

The Director hoped that this blatant display of sycophancy might win the day. The President loved to be flattered. However, the President was not to be dissuaded.

"Thank you for your concern, Gerald, but I haven't just gone through a rather unpleasant decontamination process just to look at the thing through a pane of glass."

No amount of cajoling or protests, by the JPL Director or the President's own staff could persuade the President that he should be satisfied with simply looking at Voyager One from a safe distance. The President was determined.

"The spaceship has been decontaminated to the fullest extent possible, yes?"

The Director was forced to concede that it had been. The President continued.

"And I have been decontaminated to the fullest extent possible, yes?"

"Yes, but Mr President."

"And this protective suit I'm wearing is the best there is. State-of-the-art, yes?"

"Yes. Mr President, but –."

"Then that's good enough for me. Let's go in."

The President nodded to a member of the laboratory staff to open the door and then walked into the room, making a bee-line towards the probe, feeling very happy with himself. He spent about five minutes strolling around Voyager One, examining the spacecraft and nodding to himself occasionally, trying to give the impression that he understood what he was looking at. He returned to the waiting group with a huge smile on his face. He enjoyed being President; it gave him the opportunity to do things that the common man or woman couldn't. And nobody could stop him. He was the only one that mattered.

Back in Dutch Harbor, Grant Schumacher was looking forward to his time off, time on dry land instead of at sea on the Alaskan Mermaid. Even though his job was tough physical work he enjoyed his it, but a month of kicking back and doing nothing – nothing fishing related anyway – was exactly what he needed. It was the end of the Pollock A season, Pollock B season didn't start until June, and he'd booked a flight to Anchorage for the next day. From there he would fly on to Seattle, where his family would be waiting at the airport for him. Unlike most trips, this time he would have a really interesting story to tell – how they had caught a fallen satellite in their nets, and how NASA had come to check it out and then had taken it away by helicopter. He made a mental note to remember to tell his teenage daughters that the scientist who had come to examine the thing was a woman; they were both interested in science and it would be good for them to know that such opportunities existed. He'd have loved to have had the opportunity to sit down and have a chat with Sitara, but she'd been far too busy for small talk. Just the fact that she was there, as a

NASA scientist, would be an inspiration to his girls.

His first night onshore was to be 'Grant time'. He'd have family responsibilities to take care of in Seattle but the first evening back on shore would be spent with his crewmates in their favourite local bar, The Norwegian Rat Saloon, before they all went their separate ways. After a long hot shower at his friend Richie's company apartment, newly clean-shaven (like most of his shipmates he had grown a bushy beard during the weeks at sea) and smelling fresh as a daisy, he made his way to join Richie and the rest of the crew. Most of the fishing vessels had already docked a couple of weeks earlier, offloaded their catches, and flooded the town with hundreds of noisy raucous fishermen wanting to let off steam. And most of those had already gone home. The trawler-men had all spent weeks at sea, risking their lives in the pursuit of the American dollar and, much like the cowboys of the old West returning from a cattle drive, they could be quite a handful at times. But that night the twenty-six officer strong Unalaska Police Department would have a much easier time. The town bars would be busy but, without the weight of numbers adding to the stress and confusion, the police patrols could almost relax.

Grant left Richie's apartment later than intended, having been delayed by a video call from his wife Nadine just as he was about to leave, and they'd chatted via WhatsApp for nearly half an hour. Then, his daughters wanted to talk with him, even though they'd see him the next day. Family was more important than missing out on a couple of beers.

Arriving at the Unalaskan bar, he walked over to a group of tables near the bar where Richie and several others of their shipmates were sitting. The table was already crowded with both full and empty bottles of Wild Blue lager. Richie raised a newly opened bottle of beer while handing another to Grant.

"You're late Grant. You've got a fair bit of catching up to do."

Grant took a swig of Wild Blue and looked at the plates on the table that betrayed that his friends had already eaten, as well as having a head start on him in the beer-drinking stakes. His stomach rumbled and reminded him that it needed attention.

"I've got to get some food inside me first, Rich. I'm starving."

He ordered himself a Thor Burger. If Angus beef, pulled pork, molasses BBQ and onion rings didn't silence his stomach, nothing would. There were two main reasons why Grant liked The Norwegian Rat. First, he thought the burgers were to die for and second, after spending weeks at sea with only his male shipmates to look at, it was a welcome relief to be able to see some pretty female faces behind the bar. The fact that the women were both friendly and good at their job was a bonus. However, he was very happily married and would never dream of straying.

The main topic of conversation in the bar that night – between games of pool and shuffleboard –

was, understandably, the satellite. The crew were perfectly happy with Sitara's explanation and didn't doubt her when she said that it was a reasonably common event. The trawler's skipper, Dean Romanski, a scrupulously fair man, had already assured the men that any reward for finding the satellite would be shared equally and, although they hadn't received any money yet (and had no real idea how much it would be), they couldn't help spending it in their heads. Some would spend it on new cars, some on vacations, some on house improvements, but Grant knew what his share would go on. With two teenage daughters who both wanted to study science at college, what better cause than their college fees? And, if there was some money left over, then maybe a family vacation to Disney World. The girls had always wanted to go and now, perhaps, they'd be able to take that dream holiday. But education came first.

Grant and his friends sentenced forty-seven people to death in the bar that night. They didn't want to kill them, and they had no idea that they had done so, but the fact that they'd celebrated in the company of others that night had sealed the fate of those forty-seven residents of Amaknak Island.

DAY FOUR – 27 APRIL

Infected 1,405 Dead 0

Alaska Airlines flight AS3299 from Tom Madson Airport left on time the next day, at 12:40 prompt. The take-off was uneventful, despite the runway being bordered by a large hill on one side and a steep drop off to the ocean on the other. For the first time visitor, it could be a slightly unnerving experience, but both the pilot and Grant had taken off from Dutch Harbor many times previously. Half the passengers on the Saab 2000 turboprop aircraft were from the Alaskan Mermaid and most were still nursing the remnants of the morning's hangovers. Grant, however, was surprised how little he was suffering, and settled down to while away the two and a half hour flight to Anchorage by reading the latest issue of The Bristol Bay Times. Most of his shipmates slept, trying to quell the thump-thump-thumping in their heads with the relief of unconsciousness.

By the time the plane landed at Anchorage International Airport, at 15:05 local time, twenty more passengers and the flight crew had been unwittingly served a death sentence.

Grant was now faced with a wait of nearly seven hours before his flight to Seattle – a long time to spend in an airport lounge, even if the airport was modern and had good facilities. He could have rented a car and visited Lake Hood or driven south on the Seward Highway along the Turnagin Arm, taking in the beautiful scenery, but that was the kind of thing he liked to do with his family. So he did what he normally did and took a taxi to downtown Anchorage.

He made his way straight to the 5th Avenue Mall, to begin his rehabilitation to civilisation. He enjoyed the remoteness of Dutch Harbor and the challenge and hard work of the weeks at sea, but it felt good to return to the land of Starbucks, Foot Locker, and the Apple Store. While at the mall, he bought a couple of designer fleeces for the girls (they could never have too many fleeces) and a beautiful pair of elegant gold earrings for Nadine. They had a wedding to go to in two weeks' time and he thought that they'd go well with whatever dress she decided to buy for the event. He'd have loved to have surprised her with a new dress, but that was something best bought together. It was a dangerous business for a man to buy a dress for a woman in her absence, so he'd wait until they could go shop together back in Seattle. A succulent steak at Sullivan's Steakhouse finished off the evening well, giving him plenty of time to return to the airport and catch his flight back home.

Alaska Airlines flight AS106 took off on time at 21:50, and had a perfectly smooth journey to Seattle, leaving hundreds more walking dead back in Anchorage.

DAY FIVE – 28 APRIL

Infected 6,948 Dead 0

Flight AS106 landed at Seattle at 02:16 the following morning, just four minutes late. Grant made his way through the baggage claim area and his spirits lifted when he saw his family waiting for him in the arrivals area. They waved and quickly moved to where the metal barriers opened up, allowing the arriving passengers to funnel through. Grant's youngest, thirteen-year-old Carol-Anne, ran forward and launched herself at her father. She hadn't seen him for four months, except on Skype, and couldn't wait any longer for one of his strong hugs. Grant carried her towards Nadine and his other daughter, fifteen-year-old Melody, placing Carol-Anne gently back on her feet alongside the rest of his family. After a welcome hug and kiss from Melody, it was Nadine's turn. She wasn't jealous of her daughters being greeted first – she knew that her real welcome would be far more intimate and passionate. The family would have her husband back for four whole weeks; that's what was important.

DAY SIX – 29 APRIL

Infected 8,327 Dead 0

The first breakfast of the first full day after Grant's return home from Dutch Harbor had become a Schumacher family tradition. The family got up late and headed to the Portage Bay Cafe at Ballard for brunch. Unusually, all four of them decided to eat the same meal of West Coast Benedict on organic house-made, Yukon gold English muffins, with organic, herb roasted potatoes. Carol-Anne would normally have chosen a few items from the children's menu, but now she had turned thirteen she wanted to show off her new maturity by eating what the rest of the family chose.

After eating they made their way to Washington Park Arboretum for a relaxing stroll amongst the trees and shrubs. They'd visited many times before – whenever Grant returned home – but it never lost its charm, and was exactly what Grant needed after spending so long away at sea. Strolling around the 230 acres of woodlands and gardens was the perfect antidote to his working life in Alaska. The recently opened Cascadia Forest, which covered nearly two acres, was very impressive. Despite her adult brunch earlier on, Carole-Anne showed that she was still just a kid by racing the others to the circular rock overlook, the highest elevation point in the Arboretum. She stood at the top, her hands raised proudly, drinking in the moment of her victory, and accepting the applause of an imaginary crowd of spectators. It made Grant and Nadine so happy to see that their youngest daughter was still just a child at heart - children seemed to grow up so quickly nowadays and they wanted those days of childhood to last a little longer, even though they knew from their experience with Melody that she would soon turn into a young woman.

Back home, the evening was time to just be a family, chilling out and watching a movie or maybe even binge-watching a TV series on Netflix. Pizzas were ordered and the family settled down, the parents snuggled together on the sofa, and the girls each almost swallowed by their giant bean bags. Grant could never understand the animosity of some people to having pineapple on a pizza – as far as he was concerned, you couldn't beat a deep pan Hawaiian pizza. It was the pizza of the gods.

The Schumachers knew that their time together was going to whip by faster than they would have wished and they were determined to make the most of the next few weeks. That first day was going to be the start of some wonderful family time.

DAY SEVEN – 30 APRIL

Infected 41,745 Dead 0

On his second full day back in Seattle, Grant woke up with a splitting headache, the like of which he had never suffered before. Normally a very healthy person, he tried to sleep it off but, when it intensified after a couple more hours sleep, he could bear it no more.

"Nadine. It's getting worse."

His wife rushed to his bedside, really worried. This was completely out of character for her husband. He didn't normally even succumb to a cold. She put his normal good health down to the extreme conditions that he worked in, believing that he had somehow built up a natural resistance to illnesses. This was so not like him. She put her hand to his brow.

"Christ, Grant. You're burning up. We've got to get you some medical attention. This isn't normal – especially for you."

Grant didn't like bothering doctors.

"I'll take a couple of Tylenol. That'll probably fix it."

"A couple of pills won't sort this one out, Grant. I'm taking you to a clinic. And don't try talking me out of it. I'm in charge."

Reluctantly, Grant surrendered to his wife's advice. He was in no condition to drive, so Nadine drove him to UW Harborview.

The staff at the hospital did their best to help Grant but, unable to find any specific root cause, the best that they could offer was a prescription for strong painkillers that would hopefully solve the problem.

Grant survived another six hours, his condition worsening with each passing minute, as the disease secured its grip on his body. After a painful deterioration into agony, during which he lost control of his bodily functions, he finally succumbed to his inevitable fate, nestled in the arms of his loving wife.

Elsewhere, in various towns and cities in the USA, as well as some who actually lived in Dutch Harbor, Grant's shipmates were also falling ill and succumbing to the Grim Reaper's welcoming arms. In Anchorage, both the crew of the helicopter that had retrieved the space probe from the sea and the crew of the USAF transport plane that had ferried it to JPL Pasadena were admitted to the J-BER hospital, suffering from the same symptoms, and dying in the same agony.

Sitara felt fine.

DAY EIGHT – 1 MAY

Infected 208,803 Dead 39

Thirty-nine people had died the previous day but suspicions of anything more than a local viral outbreak hadn't been aroused. It was certainly strange that twenty people had died in the same way, all in the same area, but the other nineteen victims were spread far and wide and there was no reason to consider them to be linked to the outbreak in Dutch Harbor. However, as a precaution, the Mayor of Unalaska had hurriedly convened an extraordinary meeting of the City Council in the morning of the 31st, where, despite some objections from the occupants of City Council seats C and F (who were understandably concerned for the effect that any such precaution might have on the commercial fishing industry), common sense prevailed and Tom Madsen airport was temporarily closed, in accordance with CDC recommendations. Coupled with this was the closure of the port, and vessels were allowed to neither enter nor leave the harbour. The residents were, for the most part, accepting of the measures, believing that although the closures were officially until further notice, both the airport and seaport would reopen in a matter of days.

In Washington DC, Administrator Healey and dozens of NASA staff were rushed to various city hospitals, all suffering from the same severe headaches and presenting with strange red marks on their skin. The condition of each of them deteriorated rapidly as their bodies began to rebel against them, evacuating bodily fluids at their leisure.

Deputy Administrator Nelson stayed at NASA HQ, although he wished that he could have gone to the hospital with his friend Tony, to offer moral support if nothing else. But somebody had to take charge while the Administrator was incapacitated. He knew things looked bad, but he hoped and prayed that Tony would recover and that they would soon be back together trying to solve the enigma that was Voyager One.

At 1:30 pm precisely, his office phone rang. He picked up the receiver, fearing the worst.

"Deputy Administrator Nelson, speaking."

"Sir, This is the Walter Reed National Military Medical Center. I'm sorry but I have some bad news for you."

Roger Nelson braced himself. The voice continued.

"Deputy Administrator Nelson, I'm afraid Administrator Healey passed away thirty minutes ago. We tried to make his last few hours as comfortable as possible."

Roger Nelson leaned forward in his chair, unwilling to believe what he had just been told. He had been expecting such a call, but nothing prepares a man for the news that his best friend has died.

"Thank you for letting me know. Has his family been informed?"

"Yes, sir. They were the first to be told."

The Deputy silently admonished himself for asking such a foolish question. Of course, Tony's family would have been told first. The voice had more bad news.

"I'm afraid we've lost most of the other members of your staff who were hospitalized too."

The Deputy Administrator thanked the caller and put the phone down on his desk, sitting ashen-faced looking into space until he suddenly became aware of a tiny voice trying to attract his attention. He returned the receiver to his ear.

"I'm sorry. I needed a few seconds to take in what you just told me. Do you have any idea what killed him? I mean, with the others dying as well – it has to be some kind of infection, doesn't it?"

"Of course, sir. I understand. We've called the CDC and they're sending over a team of infectious disease specialists as we speak. They should arrive soon. In the meantime, I'm afraid you're going to have to put the establishment on lockdown. Nobody in and nobody out. Except for the CDC team of course."

"Understood. Thank you for telling me."

"I just wish that I could have given you better news, sir. I'll say goodbye now. Don't forget the lockdown."

As soon as the phone call was over, the lockdown was put in place. Everybody was nervous but did as they were ordered and took the sudden imprisonment pretty well. There were far worse places to be locked in than NASA HQ.

DAY NINE – 2 MAY

Infected 1,043,750 Dead 163

Acting Administrator Nelson sat behind his desk, the desk that Tony Healey had occupied until the previous day, his head in his hands. What was he to do? What was humanity to do? Was this to be the final act of mankind's appearance on the cosmic stage? His investigators had come up with nothing to explain Voyager's presence on the planet, and it wasn't for the want of trying. They'd been over the vehicle with a fine forensic toothcomb, but to no avail, finding only Jonas Wade's DNA. With the lack of empirical evidence, the best available metaphysical minds were set to work in the hunt for an explanation. Any and all suggestions were considered, no matter how ludicrous they appeared. In the absence of any other convincing explanation, the seemingly absurd extra-terrestrial interference conclusion had become acceptable. The search for extra-terrestrial intelligence had been ongoing since the invention of the radio back in the 1900s. Could this be first contact? Could this be first *and* last contact? How else could it all be explained? All the pieces fell into place. It had always been anticipated that an alien being that came into contact with either of the two Voyagers, would be far in advance of where humanity was when the probes were launched. It was perfectly feasible that an alien might have teleportation technology, even though that was way beyond human ability at the moment. Nothing in the laws of physics forbade the transportation of large objects - even humans – but, in contemporary practice, it was an almost impossible feat. An atom had been transported three metres in 2014, but that was as far as research had got. And that didn't explain the continued existence of Voyager One out in interstellar space. Just trying to wrap one's head around the concepts was enough to cause a headache.

Suddenly David Bowie singing the first few lines of 'Space Oddity' brought Roger back to the real world. He accepted his cell phone's call.

"Deputy Administrator Nelson."

The voice at the other end of the phone identified herself as Dr Jeanette Whitty, from JPL.

"Deputy - I mean Acting Administrator Nelson. I think you should come here, to the lab, as soon as possible."

"Can't you just tell me what's happened?"

"I really think you should see for yourself, sir."

Roger Nelson wasn't really in the mood to go anywhere - the weight of the world's problems was sitting heavily on his shoulders, but he also knew that this was part of his job. He reluctantly boarded a helicopter which took him straight to the JPL complex.

A few hours later he and Dr Whitty were making their way down a corridor leading to the space probe's temporary home, In spite of the circumstances, he was quite looking forward to his first physical glimpse of what was ostensibly Voyager One.

"So, doctor. What will I be looking at?"

Jeanette Whitty sidestepped the question.

"I think it's best that you see for yourself."

Three minutes later, the pair were donning NASA Augmented protective suits before passing through the airlock and entering the large chamber where Voyager One was being examined. Roger Nelson tipped his head back and closed his eyes for a few seconds, before opening them again to confirm what he was looking at. He thought he must be dreaming, but couldn't pinch himself through the protective covering of his protective splash-suit. It was a few more seconds before he was able to speak.

"Where is it?"

Professor Whitty looked at the empty space before them, a space that had, until nearly an hour earlier, been occupied by Voyager One.

"We have no idea. One minute it was there, the next it was gone. Disappeared. It's just lucky that nobody was on it when it vanished."

Roger Nelson moved to the middle of the room.

He should have collided with the spacecraft, but there was no longer a spacecraft to collide with.

"Things don't just disappear. Not in real life. It's not Vegas. It's not a David Blaine illusion. This is NASA. We're scientists, not magicians."

Roger stopped talking, realising that he was in danger of babbling, but surely the sudden disappearance of a space probe was justification for a babble or two. Professor Whitty touched his arm.

"That's why I thought it important that you see for yourself, Sir. It's impossible, but it's happened. Voyager One has disappeared into thin air."

Back home, Roger needed some space and time to think. His best friend had died the previous day and he'd been thrust unexpectedly into the highest position at NASA. It wasn't that he wasn't capable of doing the job – he'd stood in for Administrator Healey on numerous occasions – but now the buck stopped at *his* desk. He decided to catch a couple of hours of light sleep to recharge his batteries as he'd be no good to anyone if he were too exhausted to think straight. His mind and body obviously needed a break, and he'd left instructions to call him if there were any new developments, so he didn't feel guilty for trying to take a brief nap. However, he'd hardly slept at all the previous night and the need for a more substantial sleep caught up with him, sending him into a deep slumber for several hours.

Suddenly his bedside phone rang loudly. He picked up the receiver, only to hear a very anxious voice at the other end.

"Hello? Acting Administrator Nelson?"

"Speaking."

The voice echoed Professor Whitty's initial request.

"I think you should come to Voyager Mission control, Sir."

Roger Nelson was definitely not in the mood to go anywhere else now.

"Just tell me."

The voice audibly gulped.

"Voyager One - the one that's still out there - it's gone offline. It's disappeared."

"What do you mean it's gone offline?"

The voice took a deep breath.

"Well, it takes approximately seventeen hours to receive a message from Voyager One, to confirm that the space probe is still active. It appears to have stopped sending coordinates."

Roger Nelson's heart sunk. as he realised the ramifications of this latest piece of news; both Voyager Ones had disappeared. This couldn't be a coincidence.

Two weeks earlier, over 13 billion miles away in the distant depths of space, Voyager One had been imprisoned by a tractor beam emanating from an alien spacecraft. The probe had made First Contact, and both space vehicles were now travelling in tandem, locked together by an invisible cord of light, moving further and further away from Earth at a speed of around 11 miles per second. Nothing untoward registered on the Deep Space Network monitors so nobody had any idea that anything was amiss. To the casual observer, the alien spaceship would have looked like a giant ball bearing, although it was actually a sphere within a sphere, packed with technology far superior to that of the human race. Its outer shell rotated at just the right speed to create artificial gravity inside the vessel to match that on their home planet, Argonorian 3, allowing those inside to walk around and function in just the same way as they did on their own planet.

Seventeen Earth hours earlier, on the bridge of the spaceship, an Argon commander bellowed an order.

"*Aodnot itirob ay atkert asas.*"

Released from the tractor beam's bonds, Voyager One began to drift away from the Argon vessel. Once it had reached a safe distance, the commander issued a second order, and the space probe vanished, it's billions of molecules dispersed into the void of space by a powerful blast from a weapon the likes of which no human had ever seen. Its earthbound doppelganger had no choice but to do the same.

At the White House, the President of the United States was standing in the Oval Office, discussing policy with his Vice-President and the Secretary of State, when suddenly a searing pain shot through his head like a thunderbolt, finally coming to rest behind his right eye and pounding on the rear of his eyeball.

He became visibly unsteady on his feet and was forced to sink back down into the large leather executive chair that sat behind the Resolute desk. The Vice-President rushed forward to offer support if needed.

"Mr President, are you OK?"

The President held his right hand to cover his throbbing eye and motioned with his left hand.

"A sudden headache, Andrew. I'm sure it will pass."

The Secretary of State was unconvinced.

"Perhaps we should call a doctor, Mr President."

"No need for that. Robert. It's improving already."

The pain subsided and the President meant to take just a sip of water but found himself drinking the whole glassful, cupping the glass in both hands. He stood up again, an act that concerned the two politicians; they thought that he should stay seated, at least. The President adjusted his tie and went to speak. Without warning, another shard of pain pierced his brain, worse than the first one, and he collapsed to the floor. The Secretary of State wasted no time in summoning the White House Medical Unit. Within a couple of minutes, a medic was at the President's side. He turned to the two senior members of the Administration.

"I can't tell what's caused this collapse here. We need to get him to the Urgent Care Center."

Two more medics arrived with a gurney and the President was quickly placed on board and whisked away to the White House Medical Suite, leaving the Vice-President and the Secretary of State alone in the Oval Office, neither man wishing to voice what they were both thinking. The death toll from the disease outbreak had risen to four hundred and twenty-six during the morning and showed no sign of abating. The Secretary of State spoke first.

"Do you think…?"

The Vice-President shook his head.

"I'm sure it's not."

"But are you sure?"

"Of course I'm not sure. But I don't want to think about it."

"But you – we – have to think about it. We can't ignore it."

"Let's cross that bridge when we come to it."

"I think we're going to have to cross that bridge. And sooner than we want to."

The Vice-President knew exactly what bridge the Secretary of State was referring to. If this sudden illness of the President was the portent of something worse, that the President's condition worsened, perhaps to the point where he could no longer perform his official duties, the 25th Amendment would be invoked and the Vice-President would be expected to serve as acting president until such time as the President was able to resume his duties. He wanted to go to the medical suite to see how the country's leader was doing but he also knew that he needed to be available to help the rest of the administration deal with the situation.

The President did not improve. The medical staff and facilities at the White House were the best that the nation could provide, but when the red wheals began to start showing on his body, everybody understood that the President would not recover. Although most of the cases were to be found in the United States, similar cases were beginning to show up in dozens of diverse locations around the world. The disease, whatever it was, appeared to have an incubation period of seven days when it was highly infectious but during that time those infected showed no symptoms of illness. In fact, paradoxically, many felt healthier than they had felt for a long time. Those seven days had been critical to the spread of the disease. People had crisscrossed the globe, innocent and unwitting harbingers of death, Even those who would be found immune from the disease acted as seven-day carriers of its fatal payload.

The Vice-President was sworn in as soon as it was confirmed that the President was dying. There was no point in waiting until he had breathed his last breath; he would never lead the nation again. The first thing the new President did was to declare a State of Emergency, which closed the borders and blocked both domestic and international air travel. In conjunction with the World Health Organisation, identical measures were taken by those nations that had suffered deaths through similar circumstances.

Of course, these emergency measures were not without consequences. Suddenly thousands of US citizens found themselves trapped in foreign lands.

US Embassy switchboards and internet servers collapsed under the strain of panicking Americans trying to get help, and what help there was, it was limited. Urgent messages could be sent to families and friends back in the United States, funds to help the stranded citizens could be transferred and even subsistence loans given if necessary. But, due to legal restrictions, the U.S. Department of State couldn't provide private U.S. citizens with food, water, medications, supplies, or medical treatment.

The President of the United States of America was the six hundred and seventy-sixth victim of the disease to die, and the numbers were still rising.

DAY TEN – 3 MAY

Infected 5,218,658 Dead 817

As the clock struck midnight, the number of dead rose to eight hundred and seventeen, the majority of the fatalities being in the Seattle and Washington DC areas, although there was now a steady stream of reports from all over the country of fatalities and people presenting at hospitals and clinics with the same symptoms. Nobody had any idea of how many people had been infected with the disease, although the authorities believed that the number could stretch into millions. This was hidden from the public – it would only serve to exacerbate the problem, magnifying the fear in an already panicking population.

At the crack of dawn, Seattle and DC began to witness looting and violence, as hordes of people broke into pharmacies and supermarkets, searching for any medication that could possibly provide protection against or maybe even cure the disease.

Shop shelves were stripped of their wares by desperate people determined to stockpile food and water in an effort to survive while sitting the emergency out. When pharmacies could no longer provide medications, the looters moved on to stealing them from clinics, hospitals, and veterinary practices.

Roads in and out of the cities were congested as the tarmac arteries filled up with people trying to leave their homes by car. An irrational belief spread through communities that they could outrun the disease, but that just made the situation worse, as the fleeing families carried the virus with them. Ambulances and emergency vehicles were unable to get to and from hospitals and many people died from causes totally unrelated to the pandemic, simply because they didn't receive medical attention in time.

A computer program data mined all relevant information and concluded that Ground zero was Dutch Harbor, and, more specifically, the crew of the F/V Alaskan Mermaid. The Unalaska City Council had acted promptly and taken the correct measures in quarantining the town, but unfortunately, the precautions were too late – the disease had already been allowed to escape. There had been nothing that anyone could have done to prevent this pandemic; nobody had even felt ill until seven days after the virus had infected them.

Anybody who had been on the Alaskan Mermaid on that fateful night had been infected, and a digital search was made to confirm the status of the crew of both the trawler and the helicopter that had retrieved

Voyager One. As expected, everybody had fallen prey to the disease and died – except one. Doctor Sitara Khan.

Sitara was just about to start eating her lunch when two dark-suited men approached her table in the cafeteria at NASA HQ in Washington DC. She'd wanted to go back to her own lab at JPL back in Pasadena but was now under strict orders to remain in Washington DC. One of the men took a document from his inside jacket pocket.

"Miss Khan? Miss Sitara Khan?"

Sitara put her cutlery back on the table.

"Doctor Sitara Khan. Yes, that's me. How can I help you?"

The Secret Service agent unfolded the document.

"Doctor Sitara Khan, the President of the United States of America hereby authorises your Federal isolation and quarantine under section 361 of the Public Health Service Act (42 U.S. Code §264). You need to accompany us to the National Institute of Health Special Clinical Studies Unit in the city of Bethesda, Maryland. Will you please come with us?"

Understandably, Sitara was taken aback at this unexpected interruption to her mealtime.

"Am I under arrest, agent?"

"I'm Federal Agent Steve Barber and my colleague is Federal Agent Don Hathaway. No Doctor Khan, you are not under arrest."

"So can I say no, Steve?"

"No Doctor Khan, you may not refuse to come

with us."

"May I finish my meal?"

"Sorry Doctor Khan. You need to come with us now. You can eat at the NIH campus."

Although the warrant strayed a little from the main intention of the Act, it was actually unnecessary, as Sitara understood completely the ramifications of her apparent immunity. She'd already suggested to Acting Administrator Nelson that she should undergo medical scrutiny. She stood up and started to leave the room. Agent Barber walked alongside her.

"Thank you for your cooperation, Doctor Khan."

Sitara smiled at him.

"You only had to ask,"

She thought that they would be going to Bethesda by car, but the Agent Barber explained that the roads out of Washington DC, like most cities, had been closed and people were now turning around and driving back to their homes. Instead, the three of them took the elevator to the helipad on the roof of the building, where a helicopter was waiting to take them to the NIH campus.

Later that night the new President (formally the Vice-President), the Speaker of the House, the Senate President, the Secretary of State, and the Secretary of the Treasury all died, leaving the Secretary of Defense in charge of the nation. Ironically, this pandemic was one enemy that he couldn't defeat by military means, leaving him feeling powerless in probably the most powerful position in the world.

DAY ELEVEN – 4 MAY

Infected 26,093,715 Dead 40,915

The visor of the canary yellow hazmat helmet misted up momentarily as Nolan stood by the bed, looking into the vacant lifeless eyes of the woman, imagining how beautiful she must have been when she was alive. Of course, her beauty hadn't suddenly disappeared in a puff of smoke when she had died three hours earlier, but the vibrancy that would have accompanied it was now missing. He called out to his colleague who was in the living room.

"Who was she, Triggs?"

Daniel Trigger, looking at two dead teenage girls who had spent their dying moments huddled together on the sofa, checked the address on his tablet.

"The MILF? She's Nadine Shumacher and these two beauties are fifteen-year-old Melody Schumacher and thirteen-year-old Carole-Anne. Says here, the father, Grant Schumacher died four days ago. Same symptoms."

Nolan would have preferred to have been working with anyone else but Triggs, but he had no say in the matter. Triggs was way too disrespectful to the dead for his liking.

Triggs pushed Melody's body to the side of the sofa, making space enough for him to sit between the two girls. Once seated comfortably, he took his cellphone from a pouch on the left leg of his hazmat suit and stretched his arm out in front of him to take a selfie. He stopped for a moment, rearranged the girls' bodies so that it looked like they were snuggling up to him, and took a photo. He then joined his partner in the main bedroom. Nolan shook his head.

"She must've died first. Otherwise, she'd've probably been with the girls. She probably left them watching TV in the living room so they didn't have to see her die."

Triggs moved to the foot of the bed, stepping over Nadine's soiled jeans that she had removed and tossed onto the floor when they had become too caked with human waste, and pulled her body down the bed towards him, Nolan didn't like the direction that this was taking.

"What the fuck are you doing, Triggs? Let's bag 'em up and get them out of here."

Triggs ignored his companion and instead threw his phone towards Nolan, who instinctively caught it, much against his wishes. Triggs removed his hazmat helmet and nodded at Nadine's body.

"Take a photo for me, Nolan."

Nolan couldn't believe what was happening.

"No way am I taking a photo. And for fuck's sake, put your helmet back on. You got a death wish or something?

Triggs ignored Nolan's disgust, opened his mouth and let tongue dart in and out between his lips like a snake sucking information from the air around him. Nolan's face looked like thunder.

"I'm warning you, man –"

Triggs hooked his forefingers around the waist of Nadine's stained lacy white panties and went to pull them down but was hurled backwards as a fist suddenly came out of nowhere and delivered searing pain just under his nose. Nolan stood before his workmate, who was picking himself up off the bedroom floor.

"I warned you man. You can't treat people like that. I don't know who raised your ass, but it certainly wasn't a God-fearing woman like my mama. A pack of dogs, maybe, from what I've seen. You don't treat women like that. Dead or alive, you don't treat 'em like that."

Triggs wiped blood from his split lip.

"It's just a bit of fun. She wouldn't complain. I've always wanted to fuck a woman as good lookin' as she is."

Nolan closed his eyes and shook his head."

"You're a sick SOB, Triggs. Ain't no call for that kind of thing."

Closing his eyes, even for a moment, was a mistake that Nolan would regret for the rest of his life. Triggs punched him in the stomach with all the force that he could muster. Nolan doubled over, and Triggs's knee came up and struck him square in the jaw. Nolan was still wearing his helmet, but it was designed to give protection against microbes and germs, not a physical attack. As he wavered unsteadily, Triggs ripped off his colleague's helmet, linked his hands into one conjoined fist and brought it down heavily onto the back of Nolan's neck. Nolan, now almost unconscious, could do nothing more to protect Nadine's dignity, but the adrenaline of the fight had replaced Triggs's lascivious sexual desire with bloodlust. He looked around the room for a weapon and his eyes rested upon a heavy-looking statuette on the dressing-table. He picked it up and felt the weight in his hand. It was perfect. He walked over to Nolan who was trying to get to his feet, although still very groggy. Triggs raised the statuette above his head and brought it down hard onto Nolan's skull, again and again, always in the same spot, until he heard the splintering of bone and his partner slumped to the floor, all life beaten out of him, lying in an expanding pool of his own blood.

Triggs pulled his hazmat helmet back over his head and went out to their van that was parked at the front of the house, and returned with four black body-bags. He opened up one of the body bags and clumsily pulled Melody off the sofa by her feet. Her body made a loud thump as she slumped onto the floor, leaving an ugly diarrhoea stain on the seat cushion. Triggs smirked.

"That stain won't never come out."

Melody was now laying on the floor in an undignified pose, limbs twisted at strange angles.

Nolan rearranged her arms and legs so that she no longer looked like a Barbie doll that had been tortured by a two-year-old.

"OK, Triggs. Let's zip this one up."

He took hold of Melody's legs and placed them into the body-bag, then he grabbed underneath her armpits, lifting her more gently than one might expect into the body bag. He pulled the zipper closed.

"One down, three to go."

He repeated the process with Carole-Anne and placed her beside her sister. Then he searched the house, looking for money and jewellery, before picking up the two remaining unoccupied body-bags and returning to the main bedroom, where the corpses of Nadine and her would-be protector were still where he had left them. Triggs counted his booty.

"Not a lot here, Triggs. Just some cash. Three hundred and twenty-five bucks and some change. It'll have to do."

He dropped the empty body-bags on the floor and dragged Nadine off the bed and onto one of them. She landed almost perfectly, Triggs only having to tuck her feet and head inside before sliding her engagement ring and wedding ring from her finger and putting them into his pocket. He zipped up the bag. He then carried the mother and her daughters out to the van and carelessly tossed them into the back, before going back into the house to fetch Nolan.

His partner was a good deal heavier than the women had been and it took Triggs all his strength to hoist his ex-partner's body-bag onto his shoulder and carry it outside, He opened the rear door of the van, almost dropping Nolan in the process, and then let him fall off his shoulder into the van. A couple of shoves to Nolan's feet, so that he could close the rear doors, and he was ready. He slammed the doors closed, went round to the front of the vehicle and climbed into the driver's seat.

He was supposed to take the bodies to one of the Seattle district's overworked crematoriums for instant disposal but, instead, he and his four dead passengers were going to take the I-90E out of the city. Seattle was the worst hit area at the moment, so he would head east. He had no idea what he was going to do when he got to wherever he ended up, but at least he'd be a couple of thousand miles away from the west coast. First, he had to go home and pick up his family.

He arrived at his apartment after a short drive, calling out to his family as he turned his key in the door lock.

"Carol, Shaun, Lynette? Git some bags packed. We're goin' on a road trip."

He was surprised when nobody answered him, but soon discovered the reason for the silence when he went into the bedroom. His wife, Carol, and his daughter, Lynette, were laid out on the bed just as Nadine had been, drenched in their own bodily waste. Triggs turned to the bedroom chair, where his sixteen-year-old son, Shaun, was sitting upright, his vacant eyes staring straight ahead. Triggs went over to the boy.

"Shaun. Wake up, boy. We gotta go."

The boy didn't move. Triggs slapped his son's face.

"Wake up Shaun. I knows you ain't dead. You ain't covered in shit like your ma and sister."

Triggs struck the boy again, and this time it pulled him out of his shock-induced trance. He looked at his father, life returning to his eyes.

"I couldn't do nothin' Pa. All I could do was put 'em on the bed."

Triggs showed uncharacteristic compassion for his son, leaning forward and resting his hand on the teenager's shoulder.

"You did good, son. You did good."

Shaun looked at Triggs and gave a half-smile, grateful for this rare show of affection from his father.

"What now, Pa?"

Triggs stood up.

"Now, we go on a road trip. We're headin' east, boy."

"But what about Ma and Lynette? We can't just leave 'em there."

"Look, Shaun, I've spent the last twenty-four hours picking up dead bodies – messed up bodies just like your Ma and sister – and I don't wanna do that no more. We'll leave them where they are. Won't bother 'em none."

Shaun wanted to protest but now he needed his father – such as he was – and didn't want to be left behind, so he quickly gathered up a backpack with what he considered essentials.

Twenty minutes later they were on the road, at the start of a foreboding two and a half thousand mile drive, although Shaun wasn't much impressed with the cargo of corpses that slid around the back of the van with every turn. Eventually, the constant movement got to his father too so, after a while, the van pulled over to the side of the road and father and son unceremoniously dragged the body bags out of the vehicle and dumped them by the side of the road, before continuing their journey four passengers lighter.

DAY TWELVE – 5 MAY

Infected 130,468,750 Dead 204,575

"We can't stay here for the rest of our lives. We'll go stir crazy."

Jason Green had to concede that what Patrick Dunbar was saying was true, but it would still be difficult to leave the familiarity of the neighbourhood. It had once been a thriving little community, where everybody knew everyone else and – more importantly – looked after each other. They'd managed to find just the right balance of caring for one another while still respecting the privacy of the individual, but their numbers were severely depleted now. What had once been a thriving community of over one hundred families and friends had been reduced by the plague to just Jason and the other eight adults that now sat in Patrick and Sally Dunbar's front room discussing the future, while the Dunbars' two-year-old twin daughters slept upstairs, blissfully unaware that their futures were being discussed on the floor below.

Burt Prentice, who had been born in his small

townhouse seventy-one years ago, and had lived there for the last fifty years with his wife, Mary, was reluctant to go anywhere.

"I've lived here all my life and it's never seemed like a prison to me. I like having my old furniture around me. I like having my familiar things on hand. I'm too old to start gallivanting around the country, and so is Mary."

Mary was torn between leaving and staying. She loved her little house, but she could see the logic of leaving the area too. Bottled water was in short supply now after the looting and there wouldn't be any fresh deliveries to the local stores. Drinking tap water was out of the question as the mains water supply couldn't be trusted. She knew that it would probably be a good idea to be prepared and make a move before supplies ran out. But Burt had always looked after her well, and she wouldn't challenge his opinion now, not when he needed affirmation of his role in what was left of society. He'd been the production manager at a small but busy local electrical components manufacturer and had always had an air of authority about him. Both he and Mary knew that that authority had diminished since his retirement, but he still enjoyed the respect of his community. The last thing he needed was a confrontation with his wife. Anyway, Mary sensed the majority of the people at the meeting would agree with Patrick Dunbar and if there was one thing that Burt believed in, that thing was the democratic process. He may not want to leave the area but – if the majority decided to do so – then he would do the same. He would have no choice; they both knew that there was no way that either of them could survive long without the rest of the group.

For his part, Burt's resistance to leaving the square was but a token gesture. He still played the cranky old man that the local children had considered him to be, but everybody involved knew it was just a game. In reality, he loved children and there was a mutual understanding between the local kids and the grey-haired old fellow with the handlebar moustache; a mutual affection that only masqueraded as fear. But now the only children left in the square were the Dunbar family's twin girls, Kiera and Sierra, and they were far too young to be indoctrinated into the game. He knew very well that the group would have to leave and that he and Mary would go with them. But he felt he had to keep up appearances.

Jason wanted to deal with the practicalities of their proposed journey.

"I agree that we need to move on, but where to? We can't just wander aimlessly around from pillar to post."

Marshall Franks pulled a map of the city from his pristine leather rucksack and lay it on the coffee table. The extreme edges of the map flopped over the edge of the table, but it didn't stop the group from having a more or less clear view of the layout of the city. A software engineer, the Jamaican would have felt more at home using Google Maps to present his idea, but internet access was unreliable at best and survivors of the pandemic were restricted to what was already on their laptop computers' hard drives which, in turn, depended on how long the batteries lasted. The paper map was a perfectly good substitute, so Marshall didn't see the point of wasting valuable battery life unnecessarily. The speed with which the energy and utility infrastructure had deteriorated had caught everybody off guard, and it was difficult to accept that it was just coincidence. It was almost as if it had been sabotaged. He decided to keep his conspiracy theories to himself and pointed to a location on the map.

"Jason's right. That would be pointless. However, I have a suggestion. We should make our way to the Potomac River. There's bound to be a boat there that we could commandeer – well, steal, I suppose – and head towards somewhere safer. It could be safer than using the roads. As it is, we're too vulnerable if we stay here."

Jason agreed with Marshall.

"And more importantly, we don't know what other survivors are like. They might be decent people, but they could just as easily be crazy dangerous. This disease doesn't care who it kills, and who survives seems to be down to chance. On land, we're too vulnerable, never knowing who or what might be around the next corner. At least on the water we can keep a distance between us and anyone else until we're sure of their intentions."

Xi-Wang Lin, the local pharmacist, still had

concerns.

"Say we do get to the river and manage to borrow a boat –"

His daughter, Mai, interrupted him.

"It'll hardly be borrowing a boat, dad. We're not exactly going to bring it back. Once we're out of here, we're gone."

"Please indulge me, Mai. I said borrow because it sounds so much nicer than stealing. I don't like to use the word steal. But I know we won't be bringing it back. I just feel better thinking the intention is to return it one day – however impossible that may seem now."

Marshall turned the map over to show the area surrounding the city.

"I suggest we head for DC."

The rest of the group leaned in to get a better look.

"It's the nation's capital, where all the politicians are. And who always looks after their own asses in an emergency? Senators and Congressmen. Politicians. If anywhere is set up to survive this plague, it's DC."

Burt's wife Mary nodded her head in agreement.

"I'll be sorry to leave my home, but if staying here could put us in danger, I'm ready."

Patrick Dunbar stood up and surveyed the small group of survivors.

"We've survived this long. We've seen our neighbours drop like flies and we're still here, so I think it's probably safe to assume that we're immune to the disease, whatever it is. At least we've got that in our favour. But we do need to find others like us. Other Immunes. That's another reason why we really can't stay here for much longer. We'll stagnate and maybe become complacent. That'll make us vulnerable. I suggest we use tomorrow morning to gather up supplies - food, water, clothes, and whatnot - and then set off in the afternoon. Is that OK with everyone?"

Everybody agreed with the plan – even Burt Prentice.

"Right, let's get some sleep. We've a busy day ahead of us tomorrow. Xi, I know it's kind of obvious, but can you pick out some medical supplies to take with us? I'm sure you know what stuff we should take."

"No problem, Patrick. Mai and I can make a list tonight before we go to bed."

Patrick shook everybody's hands warmly as they prepared to go home.

"Let's wake up fresh tomorrow to a world of new hope. Goodnight, everyone."

That was the cue for the neighbours to go back to their own homes to sleep in their own beds for the last time before setting off on their new adventure.

DAY THIRTEEN – 6 MAY

Infected 652,343,273 Dead 1,022,509

Sitara was dreaming of the previous year when she had visited her family in Pakistan. It had been a wonderful time, celebrating her parents' thirtieth wedding anniversary, although she hadn't much liked having to pretend that she was something that she was not. Alone with her parents, she could be herself and felt at ease, but at a semi-formal social event such as her parents' party there were certain expectations to be met – those of her parents' friends and colleagues, and she was forced to switch to a completely different personality when in public back in Pakistan. As a Muslim woman, living and working in the west, and having a foot in both camps, she was now more inclined to lean towards the lifestyle of America. Initially, the battle between her Pakistani conditioning and the desire to fit in had been a struggle, but the USA was where her future was and – barring any major upset – she would be there until her dying day. This didn't mean that she was abandoning or rejecting her Pakistani roots, but she needed to integrate with the people around her; compromises were both necessary and inevitable. She had Instagram and Facebook accounts (just as most people did) but she had two of each – one with restricted permissions for her closest and most trusted friends and one that was suitable for general consumption. She didn't like having to live her life like this, but there was no other alternative. It's how things had to be.

In her dream, she was just about to start dancing when her mind betrayed her and dragged her back to the real world, away from the festivities. Her eyes slowly opened and, when they had become accustomed to the daylight, she was forced to acknowledge the stark reality of her surroundings.

Normally, isolation was a strategy to stem the potential spread of any disease, but the numbers now were simply too large for preventative quarantine to be of any use. The world had never seen so deadly a virus spread so quickly. Now that the virus had taken hold, the wave of deaths had turned into a tsunami and had already passed the million mark. It would be much more efficient a use of CDC's facilities and dwindling manpower to discover why Sitara was unaffected by the virus and try to make projections of how many would survive the onslaught and be left to rebuild society.

Everybody who had been on or near the fishing trawler that fateful day was now dead – except for Sitara. Almost the entire population of Dutch Harbor had died. Progress had been made in classifying the disease – it was similar to the H1N1 influenza virus – but there was something different about it, something that the CDC couldn't pin down. It was more virulent and deadly than even the Spanish flu pandemic of 1918 that killed an estimated 20 to 50 million people worldwide, a third of the planet's population at the time. But the differences suggested that it hadn't originated on Earth, which was obviously a ridiculous idea.

Sitara was ensconced in an isolation suite of the National Institute of Health Special Clinical Studies Unit in the city of Bethesda, Maryland. An outsider, upon seeing all the locked doors and other security precautions, might think that she was a prisoner, but Sitara had been locked away voluntarily. She knew her immunity could be the key to creating a vaccine.

She sat up in her bed and looked through the glass pane of the entrance door, anticipating the arrival of two specially trained nurses who would want to take more of her blood. Unlike a regular hospital, it wasn't just a case of arriving at the patient's bedside, drawing the required amount of blood, and then sending it to a lab for analysis. The safety procedures were very strict and rigorously applied, and this particular part of the hospital was on lockdown; nobody could leave. Those still there were volunteers who had stayed behind to help the struggle to find a vaccine, but nobody judged those who had decided not to remain. People had families and loved ones they wished to care for, to protect, and to die alongside.

Sure enough, a couple of minutes later, Suzy Wong and Ian Petrocelli let themselves into the ante-room, which separated the main corridor from the isolation room. The ante-room was maintained at a lower pressure than that of the corridor, to prevent air from leaving and contaminating the rest of the establishment. The isolation room was similarly protected, resulting in two levels of security. The air in both her room and the ante-room was changed every three minutes, ensuring the integrity of the areas.

She watched as both nurses sanitized their hands before Ian commenced the ritual of donning protective clothing. He and Suzy were fastidious in adhering to the safety procedures, donning the slash-suit in the prescribed fashion, checking seals and the correct functioning of the air purifier. The last part of the process looked really funny. She grinned as Ian, now clad head to toe in his protective gear, performed a range of motion-fit tests to ensure that he could perform his duties unhindered by the suit. The fact that Sitara couldn't hear anything from the ante-room only added to the absurdity of seeing a so strangely garbed man bowing and doing squats, like a space-age Karate Kid warming up before a fight.

As it was the second day of Ramadan, Sitara's breakfast, her *sehri*, had been brought to her just before dawn. If her room had had a window, she could have watched the pink blush of the sunrise as the sun began to force darkness into retreat, and she said her prayer of *Fajr*, but a window would have compromised the integrity of the room so she just had to trust the clock on the wall and her intuition. She would also say the prayer of *Maghrib* at sunset, despite not having fasted during the day. These were unusual times and some flexibility was to be expected. But she didn't feel any guilt at her inability to follow the rituals correctly; things were what things were – circumstances were beyond her control. She normally only prayed in the mornings anyway, but during this sacred period, she did like to increase her prayers to the prescribed five a day.

She was a modern Muslim woman, unlike her mother who was more traditional but who – to her credit – didn't chastise her daughter for her approach to her religion. She may not have fully approved, but she recognized that the world was changing and that Sitara's life was her own and accepted her choices. Sitara loved her mother all the more for that. She didn't lie to her mother about her personal brand of Islam, but she did omit certain details. Her parents had no need to know that she had boyfriends, sometimes drank alcohol and even smoked the occasional joint. She didn't ask for forgiveness and a better life in her prayers, but rather used them as a vehicle for gratitude and love, well aware that she was living a good life of good quality and therefore Allah deserved some thanks for his blessings.

She ate her breakfast quickly, not wanting to miss the fasting deadline, even though that was a part of the ritual that she couldn't participate in this year as the taking of blood samples invalidated the fast. She didn't bother with the short prayer of opening *iftar* – there didn't seem much point if she were unable to fast - and then let the nurses perform their duties. It took hardly any time at all to draw the blood sample, unlike donning and doffing the safety equipment. Sometimes her nurses would stop by during the day for a chat, but this was always via the intercom. She wondered how much longer she would be cooped up inside the unit.

Her breakfast would be brought to her before dawn for the next thirty days – if she were there that long - and her daily routine of saying her prayers, giving blood samples, and watching movies wouldn't change. The nurses were friendly enough, and she knew that she was doing something for the greater good, but it didn't stop her from sometimes wishing that she could unlock the door and go outside for a walk, just for a while, to remind her what the outside world looked and felt like.

DAY FOURTEEN – 7 MAY

Infected and dead too many to count

Sitara had awoken at 5 am on her fourth day of isolation, the third day of Ramadan, and awaited her breakfast. She accidentally dropped back off to sleep, something she didn't realise until she suddenly woke with a start.

She looked at the clock on the wall and was shocked to see that it was nearly 6:30 am. The nurses should have brought her breakfast over an hour ago. Her rumbling stomach reminded her that her breakfast was overdue, but she was secretly grateful that she was unable to fast. At least when her food did arrive, she could eat it with a clear conscience. She went to turn on the TV, but changed her mind and decided to take a shower to freshen up instead.

After her shower, she sat up on the bed wrapped in the bath-towel. She was not only becoming anxious for something to eat, but also the clean clothes that come with the food. What was keeping the nurses? She went over to the entrance door and looked through the glass, hoping to see them donning their protective garments. She tried to open the door, but it was a pointless exercise; only hospital staff could open those doors. She tightened her towel's grip on her body and pressed her face against the glass pane, straining to get a better look at the interior of the ante-room. Everything looked normal and in its place. Suzy and Ian hadn't even entered the room yet. She told herself again that they were just late, they would come soon.

Another hour passed. Now Sitara was becoming really worried. This definitely wasn't normal. What if nobody was coming? She would be trapped. She tried to open the ante-room door again. No, don't try the entrance door. That was foolish. Try the exit door; that opened outwards. That was locked too. The doors were locked, not so much to keep Sitara inside but to keep unprotected people out. Anxiety was now in danger of giving way to panic. She told herself to calm down and think rationally. The first task – accept that nobody was coming. She was on her own. The second task – find a way out of the room.

She looked at the door. It was neither heavy nor particularly solid, as it was the difference in air pressure between the two environments that provided protection. Somehow she needed to open or break the lock. It was an electronic lock, activated by thumbprint, but she had to try something. Her rumbling stomach reminded her that death by starvation would be torturous. She tried pushing against the door. Then she tried taking a run up and barging the door, but all that resulted in was a sore shoulder. She looked around the room for anything heavy enough to make an impact. The medical equipment was state-of-the-art and too lightweight to be of any real use, so the only things that might be heavy enough to do some damage were a bedside cabinet and the bed. Sitara squatted down behind the cabinet and released the locking wheels, before pushing it with all her might into the door. There was a loud noise at the impact, but the door didn't budge. It was certainly stronger than it looked. She tried twice more, but all she succeeded in doing was damaging the door varnish.

She stared at the door and then at the bed. Perhaps the bed could do what the cabinet couldn't. Again she released the locking wheels, before manoeuvring the bed towards the door. She sighed deeply as she realized that that wasn't going to work either. If she pushed the bed at the door, it would just come to rest in front of the door, prevented from travelling any further by the wall. And there simply wasn't enough space to force the corner of the bed to strike the door with any force. She was trapped.

Sitara climbed onto the bed again and started to weep. Had she survived the pandemic only to die of starvation, imprisoned in a protective tomb?

The formally pristine white porcelain bowl was now a disgusting shade of lumpy brown, orange, and green. Suzy was on her knees, her head leaning as far as possible into the toilet bowl, trying desperately not to vomit again but failing miserably, as wave after wave of nausea overcame her body and a fresh payload of her recent meals surged from her mouth, landing with a resounding splash amongst her stomach's previously evacuated contents.

She was suddenly aware of a strange sensation, a dampening of the seat of her denim jeans. She couldn't speak, as her mouth was far too occupied with the unpleasant choice between continuing to throw up and trying to hold the vomit in. It was no contest really. The build-up in her cheeks and mouth gave her no option but to part her lips and let the offensive liquid shoot out. She gingerly moved her right arm behind her and laid the back of her hand against the centre of her bottom. She withdrew her hand quickly and looked at the wet stains that had appeared on her knuckles. She looked into the toilet bowl again. That wasn't good. She was bringing up blood now.

She wished she wasn't alone. She would have been embarrassed, of course. Nobody wants anyone to watch them throwing up and now, apparently, shitting themselves. Not under normal circumstances anyway. But these weren't normal circumstances

She didn't want to die.

But she knew that she was going to die.

Her donning buddy, Ian, had already died a few hours earlier, having shown the same symptoms. It had started with a viciously intense headache accompanied by severe pain behind his eyes and in his joints and muscles. Ian had tried to insist that it was just a mild case of the flu, but both nurses knew different. They had seen enough people succumb and die to know that a course of Gripalax pills wasn't going to sort this out.

As soon as the red wheals had erupted on his face, arms, and legs, Ian had known it was all over. He'd begged his colleague to smother him with a pillow or something, to put him out of his misery, but Suzy just couldn't bring herself to do it. She'd watched him as he spent two hours in the bathroom throwing up, just as she was now doing. She had squirmed at his embarrassment as his bowels had sporadically vacated themselves without warning, and had watched him finally struggle for breath as his lungs began to cease taking in air. She watched him die a cruel and agonising death.

She looked at the deep red marks on her own arms, wishing that she had put on a long-sleeved blouse that morning. It wouldn't have made the marks disappear but at least she wouldn't have been able to see them. She'd been on her way to her locker to fetch her favourite blouse when she had been forced to make an emergency diversion to the bathroom. That was an hour and a half ago and she hadn't left the bathroom since. But if she was going to die, she was damned if it was going to be in the bathroom.

She hauled herself to her feet and leaned against the bathroom wall. The door was open as she had felt in no condition to worry about closing it behind her when she had started vomiting. She was the only one in the recreation room anyway. The only living person, that is. Her colleague was slumped in an armchair, but he was stone cold dead. Suzy would have liked to have been able to lay him on the bed that stood in the corner, somewhere for the staff to take a nap at break-times. She would have liked to have allowed him some dignity in death but her searing headache had started about an hour before he died and she just didn't have the energy.

Suddenly she remembered that there was somebody else who needed her attention more urgently. Sitara was alone and would probably be panicking by now. If Suzy didn't let her out of the isolation room, Sitara would die – not from the virus, but a long, lingering death due to starvation. Suzy couldn't let that happen to her.

The journey from the bathroom to the isolation unit was a real effort. Suzy wanted to fall down and curl up in a ball. She wanted her mom and dad. She wanted someone, anyone to make this pain stop. She didn't want to die alone.

She managed to drag her aching, puking, shitting body through the corridors towards the isolation unit, stopping for a breather only when faced with an electronic lock to negotiate. There were three locked doors en route and each time she took a deep breath and pressed her thumb against the optic reader, sighing with relief when she heard the welcome click of the lock disengaging and the door opening. Each time she almost fell through the door and watched as it closed behind her.

The pain was almost unbearable now. It was

becoming harder and harder to breathe and she could hear herself starting to wheeze. She couldn't give up though, she didn't have that luxury.

Doing her best to ignore the pain that she was feeling in her elbows, she pressed her thumb against the reader and the door to the ante-room opened. She somehow dragged her aching body inside and heard the door close behind her. She saw the protective gear hanging in its place but looked away. There was no point in donning the equipment now – there was nothing to protect her from. She staggered over to the equipment table and picked something up, securing it tightly in her left hand, before pressing her right thumb against the fingerprint reader.

Again, she let out a sigh of relief, but not as great a sigh of relief as Sitara when she saw the door opening. Then it was a gasp of horror as Suzy fell through the doorway, this time allowing herself to collapse on the floor, preventing the door from closing again. When she saw the condition that Suzy was in, Sitara rushed over to help her but the nurse was beyond help, gasping for air, forcing herself to speak.

"Important. You must get away."

Sitara didn't know what to say, as Suzy opened her left hand to reveal a razor-sharp scalpel. She looked up at Sitara.

"Cut thumbprint off."

Sitara was horrified at the words.

"Cut thumbprint off. Opens doors."

"I can't."

"Have to. Do it now."

Sitara took the scalpel from Suzy and held it to the nurse's right thumb. She froze for a moment before her eyes welled up with tears.

"I can't. I can't do it. Can I wait until after?"

"Do it now. I...I need to know you're safe."

Sitara brought the blade close to Suzy's thumb but drew back again, unable to follow through with the grotesque task – even though she knew her life depended upon it.

"Sorry. I just can't do it."

Suzy wheezed.

"Give back."

Sitara handed the scalpel back and was forced to look away as Suzy sawed off the fleshy tip of her thumb, leaving the thumbprint intact. Her determination to release Sitara from her sterile prison trumped any pain that either the disease or the blade could throw at her. Suzy swallowed a gulp of air, as blood gushed from the wound.

"Take thumbprint. Open doors."

It was hard for her to do so, but Sitara took the bloody thumbprint from the nurse, wiping it clean on her towel. Suzy tapped Sitara's leg.

"Clothes in locker room. Open doors. Thumbprint."

It was becoming almost impossible to breathe. Sitara could do nothing to help Suzy but at least she could ensure that her nurse wouldn't die alone. Three minutes later it was all over and Suzy had gasped her last breath. Sitara leant over and kissed her on her forehead.

"Thank you, my friend. Thank you for saving my life."

She stood up and saw that the towel had several pus and bloodstains on it from where she had held Suzy, but she couldn't worry about that now. If she were to go outside she couldn't do so wrapped in a towel. She really needed some clothes. She took a few seconds to compose herself, before stepping over Suzy's corpse into the ante-room. The door to the corridor was closed but this time she had her macabre key. A sudden fear swept over her – what if the disembodied thumbprint didn't work? She delicately placed the thumbprint over the optical reader.

Nothing happened.

What could be wrong? Perhaps there wasn't enough pressure behind the print? She screwed up her face in disgust as she placed Suzy's thumbprint over that of her own and pressed it against the reader. This time the door clicked open. She rushed through to find herself in an empty corridor. Which way should she go? Left? Right? Did it matter? She saw exit signs pointing to the left and would have loved to leave the hospital straight away, but she couldn't leave the hospital wearing only the towel. She turned right, hoping that she was going the correct way.

Three more locked doors were opened, and Sitara found herself outside the recreation room. She entered but almost walked out again when she saw

Ian's corpse sat up in an armchair.

She went over to the lockers, all of which were secured by an electronic lock, each requiring the owner's thumbprint in order to gain access. Pushing her squeamishness to one side, she pressed Suzy's thumb over each of the four readers until one of the doors opened.

She looked inside. There was an e-reader tablet, a couple of paperback books, half a dozen magazines, a make-up bag, a pair of stonewashed denim jeans, a T-shirt, a pair of black lacy panties, and a pair of Nike training shoes. She was surprised at the T-shirt - Suzy hadn't seemed like a Led Zeppelin fan. She also thanked Allah that she and Suzy were more or less the same size, clothes wise at least. She turned to face away from the lifeless Ian as she let the towel drop and hurriedly put on the panties, T-shirt and jeans. She knew he was dead and that his eyes could see nothing, but she still felt an urge to protect at least some of her modesty. The T-shirt was a snug fit, but not so snug that it could cause her any embarrassment. The trainers were one size too large for her, but they would have to do. It wasn't as if she had much choice. She looked inside the locker again and found a few pairs of running socks. She put two socks on each foot in an effort to make the Nikes a better fit.

Clothed again and feeling much more comfortable, she retraced her route back to the isolation room, looking straight ahead as she passed it, so as to avoid seeing Suzy's body again. Another two doors and she was outside, taking a deep breath of fresh air and feeling the spring breeze on her face for the first time in four days.

The Clinical Health Center had been disturbingly empty as Sitara had made her way to the exit. Unbeknown to her, Ian and Suzy had been the only nurses still on campus. Everybody else, both staff and inpatients, had been sent home to die with their families. Sitara was the exception – while she was alive, there was hope. Ian and Suzy, along with a handful of research scientists had volunteered to stay behind, ignoring the urge to join their families and friends, and instead dedicating their remaining time to what they considered to be mankind's final battle. And now every one of them was dead.

The streets of Bethesda were not completely deserted. Dozens of empty cars were parked along the wide streets, waiting for drivers who would never return. Most of Bethesda's residents had returned to their homes to offer comfort and solace to each other before the inevitable wave of death overcame them. But some of those who were alone in the city had tried to pretend that nothing was wrong, that somehow by ignoring the disease they could make it all go away. The truth was that they had been terrified of dying alone.

It was the bodies of lonely people who littered the streets of the beautiful city. Sitara wished that she had been given the opportunity to experience Bethesda before it was ravaged by the plague. The bars and restaurants looked intriguing. In a different time, she would have loved to have checked out the Cava Mezze Grill, Jaleo Spanish restaurant, and Sweetgreen's, and would have tucked into a delicious sandwich from Potbelly's Sandwich Bar. But she didn't even know where her next meal was coming from.

It would have been bad enough if the bodies on the streets were simply inanimate versions of their previous selves, but each and every one of them bore the scars and marks of the torture they had faced in their final moments. The red wheals on the victims' skins were unsightly, but not enough to make Sitara turn her head away in disgust - she turned her head out of sorrow. Each and every corpse was steeped in its own waste, flies buzzing around the corpses enjoying so many impromptu meals. A few were not yet dead, finding the strength in their draining bodies to stretch an arm towards Sitara, imploring her to help them or put them out of their misery, but she could do neither.

The smell on the streets was becoming unbearable and made her gag more than once. She had to get away from all these dead and dying people, but she had no idea in which direction she should run. It didn't really make much difference – she was bound to arrive at the city limits eventually. She nearly stumbled over a young child, the bodies of his dead parents snuggled up to him, and a poodle - obviously their pet – which was wandering between the three of them, unsure of what to do next.

The sight of dead children was the worst. She passed a playground and saw the body of a young girl, slumped on a swing. A woman, face stained with tears, lay dead on the ground directly behind her. Sitara imagined that the girl's mother had probably taken her to play at the park one last time. Had she seen the life seeping out of her daughter and been unable to leave her side? Tears filled Sitara's eyes as she noticed a sticker on the child's dress, proudly proclaiming '*It's my birthday. I am five*'.

Sitara could stand it no more and let herself fall to the ground, sobbing uncontrollably. Through her tears, she could see the clear blue sky above her head. How could something so obscene take place on such a beautiful day? She shouted up to the heavens before lying down on the ground and curling up into a ball.

"How can you do this Allah? How can you let this happen?"

DAY FIFTEEN – 8 MAY

Jason Green sat in an armchair watching a DVD movie. He had a large collection of films, but it didn't make any difference which one he watched, the scenes shown on the screen bore no relation to the world. Actually, that wasn't strictly true. One film, 'I am Legend' starring Will Smith, looked exactly like the world outside. The streets were deserted and silent. No birds sang. No dogs barked. It was as if the wildlife recognized that the city was becoming a giant morgue and had decided to steer well clear of it. Jason would have liked a dog for company – even Will Smith had a dog with him in the film – but he was totally alone. If he stayed there, the outlook was for a very lonely life with no one to talk to, no living creatures anywhere. He'd been forced to stray out of his comfort zone in order to look for more provisions, but looters hadn't left much. He'd seen a few living people but they had run away as soon as they saw him, probably fearing that if they got too close, they too would become infected. If he stayed where he was, the choice appeared to be death from hunger, thirst or sheer loneliness.

He had no idea why he was still alive.

Three days earlier, Jason had been helping plan a group evacuation to find a new home with more resources, but by the following morning, he was the only one alive, having spent a restless night listening to the death throes of his neighbours.

The next day, having had hardly any sleep, he had taken it upon himself to clear up the mess – the 'mess' being the bodies of his friends. Xi-Wang Ren, the local pharmacist and his seventeen-year-old daughter Mai had been the first two that Jason dragged from their homes and placed in the now deserted square that had once been the social epicentre of the community. Then, Burt and Mary Prentice, the elderly couple from number twenty-three, had been hauled across the road to the square, where they had been placed carefully on top of the Chinese father and daughter. Jason had been surprised that the pensioners had survived as long as they had; they were obviously tougher than they looked. The Jamaican, Marshall Frank, and his website-designer Japanese wife, Sayuri, had died wrapped in each other's arms, their devoted love for each other masking the horror of their deaths. It was having to deal with this nauseating aftermath that had convinced Jason that he shouldn't stay in his home much longer. He just wanted to get away from the place, to leave the bad memories behind him. Of course, they would always be in his head but he hoped that with new surroundings and perhaps new friends, he could relegate them to the back of his mind. Removing local builder Patrick Dunbar, his wife Sally, and their twin two-year-old daughters was the straw that broke the camel's back. As he threw the bodies of the two innocent toddlers onto the small pile of bodies, the sound of their giggles invaded his mind. He didn't really have a game plan as to what he was going to do with the small heap of bodies – he couldn't burn them because the smoke might attract outsiders and that could be dangerous. Maybe he should have left the bodies where they were and saved himself a lot of distress. He also knew that if he stayed in the square, the stench of his friends' rotting carcasses would be a daily reminder of what had happened and that he was alone.

He switched off the TV and DVD player and walked across the room to where the two-stroke electric generator was still chug-chugging. He pressed the kill switch and the apartment suddenly became silent. Eerily silent. He picked up his backpack and the Remington R-15 Semi-Automatic rifle that he had 'found' in a local hunting store and headed towards his front door. He left his apartment and trotted down the two flights of stairs to the main door. Opening the door slightly, he peeked through the small gap as a precaution, although he knew that this was no guarantee that it was safe to leave. However, if he stayed at home, he would simply be living in a gilded cage until he died. No, not living. He'd be existing. Shutting himself inside a box might be the safer choice, but it certainly wouldn't be living.

He opened the door wider. Fortunately, it was quiet outside. Some might say too quiet. No birds singing. No dogs barking. A tabby cat suddenly ran across his path, startling him. If it had been a dog he may have been tempted to try to befriend it – even four-legged company would be better than none – but a cat wouldn't need him and would be a fair-weather friend.

He looked out into the street, rifle at the ready, as his eyes became accustomed to the bright sunlight again after having been enveloped in the near darkness that the closed curtains of his apartment had provided. The road was completely empty. Even the sprinting cat had disappeared out of sight. He checked his backpack and the semi-automatic rifle again. One of the side pockets of his backpack contained spare magazine clips for the rifle and the pocket on the opposite side of the bag held ammunition for the Beretta 9mm semi-automatic pistol he had holstered by his right hip. With a bullet-proof vest, he felt he was ready for anything.

The rest of the backpack was filled with 'rescued' clothes and food rations. A flashlight, a water-bottle, and a spare pair of boots hung from the buckles of the bag. Jason cautiously stepped outside and surveyed the kingdom that he was about to leave. His kingdom, population one, and about to become population zero. He turned around, pulled the door closed behind him, double-locking the door. If he needed to come back, he wanted there to be a good chance that the building would be unoccupied.

He walked for about forty-five minutes, not seeing a soul until he came across an old school building. He stayed a short distance away, just observing, trying to evaluate the characters of a small group of people who had occupied the building. They seemed harmless enough, a mixture of men, women, and children, and looked reasonably secure behind the high walls surrounding the playground. He didn't see any weapons, although that didn't mean that they didn't have any. He doubted that they would have stayed in one place like this, in a semi-secure environment that didn't offer impregnable protection, without weapons.

Suddenly he heard a sound behind him and instinct drove him to dive to his right, narrowly avoiding being hit by a bullet fired by one of two men who had crept up on him. That answered that question then – they definitely weren't friendly. Although he too was armed, he had no time to even think about defending himself with his rifle. Fight or flee are the two survival instincts, and he had been left with no choice but to make a run for it. He had to be more careful in future. He had always been a fast runner, be it sprinting or long/middle distance running, and that was what probably saved his life. He leapt to his feet and started sprinting away from the school compound, zig-zagging so that the gunmen would find him a much more difficult target to hit. He darted left and right, into roads and alleyways, bullets ricocheting around him, having no idea where he was going and not really caring either. He was athletic, but he knew that even he couldn't keep up this pace forever. The gunfire ceased, and he hoped that this was a good sign; perhaps his pursuers weren't as fit as he was and had given up the chase. Perhaps they considered that the distance between him and the school was now sufficient that any threat Jason may have posed had disappeared. He'd better get off the street. He saw a door to a warehouse. It was impossible to tell whether it was empty or not but that was the least of his concerns. Fortune looked down on him as the door wasn't locked and he ducked inside the building, closing the door behind him.

It was dark inside. Of course it was. There were only small windows, high up. Slowly his eyes became accustomed to the poor light, and he could make out the shape of several rows of tall racks packed with cardboard boxes. There was a forklift parked in one of the aisles, but he didn't feel safe enough to risk starting the engine. Just because the gunfire had stopped didn't mean that his two pursuers had gone. Perhaps they had, but he wasn't going to risk it. He chose a rack two rows down that wasn't too full of boxes, allowing him more room to climb up the structure. Standing on the wooden baseboard, two shelves up, he used his knife to open the first box. It contained packs of disposable diapers; there was no point in taking those. The next box contained packs of toilet paper. There was no way that he could take a complete pack with him – his backpack was large, but not large enough to waste valuable space with a sixteen roll pack of toilet rolls. He'd take a couple with him though, knowing that the importance of toilet rolls should never be underestimated. Another box yielded first-aid kits; now that could certainly come in useful. He was just about to open the fourth box when a noise from the far corner of the warehouse caught his attention. It was probably a mouse, or maybe even a rat, but he decided to take a look anyway. He was pretty sure that nobody else had entered the warehouse, so he didn't think it would be the men who had shot at him. He drew the pistol from its holster – just in case – and took a flashlight out of his pocket. He didn't switch it on though, silently making his way to the source of the noise.

Whatever was there was keeping very still but Jason could just about make out the sound of slow breathing. He came within five yards of the mystery creature and then pointed both the gun and the flashlight at the origin of the breathing, simultaneously switching the flashlight on.

He wasn't prepared for what he saw.

There was a man crouching underneath an empty rack, his exaggerated shadow cast on the wall behind him by the bright flashlight. The man, dressed in dark blue denim jeans, and light blue denim shirt, raised a hand in front of his face to shield his eyes from the bright light. On his feet were a pair of Adidas trainers. The man looked at Jason, a mixture of fear and curiosity evident in his eyes. Jason meant to ask the stranger who he was, but that's not what came out of his mouth.

"What are you?"

The stranger understood that Jason had the upper hand and clearly recognized the threat of the revolver that was pointing at him. Jason revised the question.

"Who are you? Come out and stand up so I can see you properly"

The stranger understood Jason's gestures and did as he was told. There was nowhere to run to anyway, and he was unarmed. Jason looked at him again.

"What's your name?"

The stranger said nothing.

"You must have a name. Everybody has a name."

Again, no response. A thought crossed Jason's mind. Perhaps the man was deaf or dumb, or perhaps he just didn't speak English. Jason asked the question in Spanish but got the same response.

"Can you hear me?"

The man looked puzzled and gestured towards his right ear, behind which was located something that looked like a hearing aid.

"So you're deaf then."

Jason was confused. The man opposite him was a man, but yet not a man. He wasn't a man like any that Jason had come across, anyway. He stood about five foot five tall, and was obviously very strong; his arms and legs, although they appeared to be a little shorter than normal, were very muscular. His head, however, seemed elongated and his brow was more pronounced than anyone's that Jason had ever seen. His nose was broad and seemed to project quite a lot from his face, but his chin was almost non-existent. His eyes were unusually large, but just the right size to fill the evidently larger eye sockets of the man, although slightly obscured by the size his brow. Was this an alien? Perhaps, but he didn't think so. This was a human, albeit a rather strange looking one. The man didn't seem to be threatening, although he was understandably nervous, which was hardly surprising really, considering his present circumstances Having got over his initial shock, Jason continued.

"My name's Jason. Jason Green."

The man pointed at Jason's mouth.

"That's my mouth."

Jason felt like he was having a conversation with a two-year-old. Jason resisted the temptation to speak in broken English. The man might look like a caveman, but he was still human. The stranger opened and closed his hand like someone might do to signify that somebody is talking too much.

"You want me to stop talking?"

The man became agitated.

"Oh. Sorry. You want me to keep talking?"

The stranger opened and closed his mouth several times, all the while pointing at Jason, who was unsure what to do.

"I don't know what you want, so I'll keep talking. If you're deaf you won't hear me anyway, so it won't matter."

Jason was pleased to have someone to talk to, even if the conversation was all in one direction. It didn't explain why the stranger didn't seem to be able to talk though. Jason had met a few deaf people in his life, and most were able to speak to some extent or another. Maybe, the stranger had been deaf and dumb from birth. That could explain his silence.

Jason spent the next hour telling his life story to his new companion. He told him about his schooldays, about his dating experiences, about the jobs he'd done in his life. He told him about his family, and about his divorce. He wasn't really sure why he told the stranger so much personal information, but the man had a kindly face and seemed to be listening intently, even though he couldn't hear Jason. The autobiography ended with Jason explaining how he had ended up in the warehouse.

"And that's my story. I wish you could tell me your story."

The man nodded and Jason nearly jumped out of his skin when he spoke to him.

"Thank you, Jason. I will tell you about myself but now is not the time. We have company."

Jason's pursuers had found him. The metal door opened and two figures stepped through the opening, silhouetted in the glare of daylight, before advancing into the darkness of the warehouse. Jason put a finger up to his lips to gesture to the stranger that he should remain silent but was surprised to see that the man had disappeared. He was on his own again.

He ducked behind a packing crate and tried not to even breathe, lest the men hear him. He watched as they made their way along the aisle between the racks, peering between the spaces, looking for their prey. Suddenly, one of the tall racks started teetering at an angle, until a dozen boxes slid off the racking and landed directly on top of the intruders, knocking them out cold. Jason emerged from his hiding place and joined his stocky saviour who was looking at the two unconscious men.

"Obviously those boxes weren't full of diapers."

He grabbed his new friend by the arm.

"Come on. We'd better get out of here. There were others who'll miss them."

Sitara had cried herself to sleep the previous night, and she was grateful that her mind had allowed her to do so, for she couldn't have taken any more stress that day. She felt like giving up and letting go of life but, clearly, that wasn't what Allah had planned for her. She'd slept right through to the next morning, waking up exactly where she had lain down in the playground. She dragged her body up off the asphalt and looked around her, hoping that yesterday had been a bad dream, but the little girl was still dead on the swing, and her mother was still dead on the ground behind her.

She started walking, looking straight ahead to avoid making eye contact with anything that wasn't within the scope of her forward vision. She had no desire now for peripheral vision; peripheral vision merely magnified the horror of her new environment. She walked for hours, like a woman possessed, ignoring the pain in her legs and the exhaustion that was creeping back into her body, lack of food taking its toll. She strode out of downtown Bethesda, through the suburbs, and onto a highway. She didn't know where she was going, but she didn't care.

Jason wasn't sure that he could trust his new companion fully, but was prepared to give him the benefit of the doubt – after all, the stranger had just saved his life. The most pressing problem at that moment was to get as far away from the area as possible. There were a number of vehicles parked outside the warehouse, and it didn't take too long to find one that had been left unlocked. Jason could never understand why many Americans still seemed to leave their cars unlocked, but he was grateful for the owner's lack of good judgement. He jumped into the driver's seat and beckoned the stranger to get in the SUV too.

"Come on. Get in. We can't waste time admiring the car."

The stranger was checking the car over and seemed particularly taken by the wheels, which amused him greatly. Jason was becoming impatient.

"What's so funny? We have to get out of here."

Jason's saviour climbed into the passenger seat.

"The vehicles of your planet have wheels."

Jason put the Chevy SUV into gear and its wheels

span for a second or two before finding traction and propelling the vehicle out of the parking lot at speed, snaking a little before settling down and accelerating along the highway. The passenger shook his head.

"We do not have that problem with our vehicles."

Jason had so many questions to ask but waited until the car was on the freeway before interrogating his passenger.

"So...I told you my name back in the warehouse. What's your name?"

"I am Enak."

"Why didn't you answer when I started talking to you back there?"

"I had nothing to say. Not because I did not want to talk to you, but because I could not. I did not understand what you were saying."

Jason pointed towards his own ear.

"I thought you were deaf. You're wearing a hearing aid. You seem to speak good English now. How did that happen?"

Enak laughed.

"It is a universal translating device."

"A translating device?"

"Yes. It looks for patterns in speech and uses them to infer the construction of the target language. That is why I wanted you to keep talking to me. It never stops learning and updating its database. It is doing so as we speak."

"OK. I can see how that would help you understand what I'm saying, but how are you able to talk to me?"

"It is connected directly to the left cerebral cortex of my brain and delivers the translation directly, so my mouth and larynx operate accordingly."

Jason was impressed. His next question was going to be somewhat tactless.

"Enak, I don't mean to give offence, but what are you?"

"I am human."

"But you found it funny that the vehicles on our planet have wheels. You said, and I quote, the vehicles of your planet have wheels. Are you from another planet?"

"I am, but I am still human."

"You do look human in some ways but in others, you don't. I mean you're basically like us – two arms, two legs etc. – but, to be brutally honest, you look like the pictures of Neanderthals that I've seen. No offence."

Enak looked confused.

"What are Neanderthals?"

"They were another species of human that used to live on Earth, but became extinct thousands and thousands of years ago."

"Ah. I think I understand. We are Argon, but perhaps you call us Neanderthal. We originate from this planet."

Jason was stunned. Was he really driving a car along the freeway, with a real live Neanderthal sitting in the passenger seat?

"Enak, but if you're a Neanderthal –"

"Argon."

"If Argons and Neanderthals are the same species, you became extinct about forty thousand years ago."

"Not extinct. We left. In fact, we were taken."

Jason's mind was abuzz. Enak's answers simply led to more questions.

"But Neanderthals were the dumb ones."

He immediately wished he hadn't said that. You don't insult someone you've just met, by calling their race, or species, or whatever, dumb. Especially if they look like they have the strength to snap your bones like a twig.

Enak laughed out loud so hard, that he was forced to hold his belly in an attempt to control himself.

"We are the dumb ones? You are still using wheels. We have perfected interstellar travel. You are still sending unmanned spacecraft to explore the universe, and you have only just got one of them to leave your solar system. I think we both know which one of us is the dumb species here – and it is not mine. I will answer more of your questions later, but now, I need to get some sleep. However, before I do, I have one question for you."

Perhaps pushing that racking over took more out of Enak than he was letting on.

"OK. But please tell me more later on. What's your question?"

Enak yawned.

"Where are we going?"

Two miles into a twelve mile stretch of Branch Avenue, the MD-5 S, Jason thought he spotted someone walking along the hard shoulder. He slowed down to take a closer look as he drove past, remembering his close escape at the warehouse and not wanting to take any unnecessary risks. As he passed the person, he looked to his right and saw that it was a young woman, unarmed and looking totally exhausted. He had a very brief debate with himself – Enak was still sleeping – and stopped the car. Slipping the vehicle into reverse gear he backed up until he was alongside the woman, who by now looked fit to drop. He wound down the driver's window.

"Hi. Can I offer you a ride?"

Sitara's initial instincts were to refuse. Her mother, like mothers the world over, had drilled into her as a child that you shouldn't accept rides from strangers, but these were extraordinary times. The fear of infection didn't cross her mind, as she was obviously immune. She really wanted to jump into the car and lock the door, to be with living human beings again, but hesitated.

"Where are you going?"

The woman looked like she wasn't deliberately going anywhere, but rather was leaving somewhere.

"To Mechanicsville. Well, close to Mechanicsville. An Amish settlement on Route 236. Where are you going?"

Sitara shrugged her shoulders.

"Nowhere really. I just knew I had to get away from Bethesda. It's full of dead people."

Jason unlocked the right-hand rear door of the car.

"You'd better get in. It's too dangerous to walk along the highway like this. Especially now."

Sitara ignored her mother's warnings and got in the car. She knew it would be difficult to survive on her own, her feet were hurting, and she had nothing better to do. Sure, this guy and his sleeping friend could be rapists and murderers but, for some reason, she had a feeling that joining them in the car was the safer option. The driver looked like a good man – whatever a good man was supposed to look like, that is. She couldn't see his friend's face, but chances were that if the driver was a good man, then his friend would be too. Jason turned towards his new guest and offered his hand.

"Hello again. I'm Jason. And Sleeping Beauty here is Enak."

Sitara accepted the handshake.

"I'm Sitara. Pleased to meet you, Jason.

Sitara's stomach gurgled.

"Sorry to be so direct, Jason, but do you have anything to eat? I'm starving. I haven't eaten for hours."

Jason took two packets of Oreos from the glove compartment.

"Not exactly a square meal, I'm afraid."

He handed the packets to Sitara, who gratefully started to eat. She continued eating while she thanked him, something that her mother wouldn't have approved of. Talking with one's mouth full was a definite failure of etiquette, but Sitara was far too hungry to worry about observing the niceties of table manners.

"Thanks for the cookies, Jason."

"No problem."

"Your friend's name is Enak? That's unusual."

Jason accelerated off the hard shoulder to continue driving along the road.

"Strange name, strange man. I've only just met him, but he seems ok. He saved my life back in Bethesda, so that's a good start. I'll introduce you properly when he wakes up. We can get something more substantial to eat too."

Sitara fastened her seatbelt and suddenly realized that she was sharing the rear seat with a semi-automatic rifle. She told herself to ignore it, it shouldn't be a surprise that these men have armed themselves – the world had become a dangerous place. In normal times she was fervently in favour of strict gun controls, but these were no longer normal times. Jason looked in the rear-view mirror and could see that Sitara's eyes kept glancing towards the rifle.

"There's a coat on the parcel shelf. You can cover it up with the coat if you like."

"Excuse me?"

"The rifle. Cover the rifle with a coat if you like. There's a coat on the rear dash. I can see the gun's bothering you. I don't like the idea of civilians having guns either, but these days you need something to protect yourself with. Not all survivors are going to be nice guys."

Sitara covered the weapon and immediately felt more relaxed.

"You're a Brit aren't you?"

"My accent gave it away, yeah?"

"I like the British accent. Kinda sophisticated."

"The accent may sound sophisticated to you Americans, but we're like anyone else."

Sitara was so glad to have someone to talk to.

"I'm from Pakistan originally, but I came to the States as a child. So why are you here?"

"I came over here a few years ago to work on an engineering project, liked it, met my wife and stayed."

"Where's your wife now?"

The delay in answering made Sitara wish she hadn't asked the question, but it was difficult to suddenly eradicate normal everyday questions from small talk.

"She died. The plague."

"I'm sorry. It was insensitive of me to ask."

"It's alright. It's not your fault. The disease has taken so many people."

Sitara suddenly felt a pang of guilt. She could well be the reason that Jason's wife was dead. She and the crew of the Alaskan Mermaid had almost certainly brought the virus back to the mainland with them. But how could she have known?

"What about your friend, Enak? What does he do?"

"I don't know. As I said, I only met him this

morning. I'll tell you one thing though. I think he's got one hell of a story to tell us."

Sitara was feeling more comfortable now, and she was glad that she had ignored her mother's advice. As the vehicle turned left onto MD-5 S/Mattawoman Beantown Road, Jason handed Sitara a bottle of Gatorade.

"Sorry, I should've offered you something to drink earlier."

Sitara took the bottle from Jason's outstretched hand.

"Thanks. I could do with that too."

"So, what were you doing in Bethesda? You live there?"

Sitara saw no need to hide anything. The two - three of them now - were obviously in the same boat, immune to the disease. She'd rather that her rescuers know that she wasn't a danger to them.

"I was at the Institute of Health. They were studying me, doing tests and what-not, to try to find out why I was immune."

"I'd like to know that too. Everyone around me died, but not me. I reckon I must be immune too."

"And your friend?"

"I don't know for sure, but I assume he's also immune."

"Anyway, I was in an isolation room, helping them try to find a vaccine when suddenly I realized that I was on my own. I was locked in the room and couldn't get out. I thought I was going to die of thirst and starvation. Suzy - one of my nurses - let me out."

"Where's Suzy now?"

"Dead."

"I'm sorry."

"I managed to get out of the hospital but all I found outside were sick people dying and corpses all over the place. The city smelled like death. I had to get out of there. So I started walking, not caring where I was going. I just had to get away from there."

Jason spotted a petrol station alongside a small outlet centre a couple of hundred yards further up the road.

"I'm going to pull in at that petrol station to see if there's any food there. We don't need fuel yet, the car already had a full tank when we picked it up, but we could do with more food – if there is any."

Sitara was also glad of the pit stop.

"I'd like to get out of these clothes too. They're not mine, they're Suzy's. There's an outlet centre next to the gas station – there's bound to be a clothes shop there.

Jason tapped Enak's arm a few times until his eyes opened.

"Don't be startled…"

Enak blinked.

"Startled?"

"Surprised. We have a guest. Enak, this is Sitara. Sitara, Enak."

Sitara couldn't help but notice that Enak's physiognomy was, to put it mildly, unusual, but she didn't say anything.

"Pleased to meet you Enak."

Jason reached back and took the rifle from underneath the coat on the rear seat.

"We'd better take this. We don't know what we're going to find in there. I just hope it's food."

Sitara reminded Jason of the other necessity.

"And clothes."

"Yes. And clothes. But we should stick together though. We don't know what or who we might find."

Jason went first, and Enak and Sitara followed behind him. The fuel stop had obviously had no visitors for a while and Jason half expected to see tumbleweed trundle across his path as they walked towards the building. He looked through the window. The place seemed empty until he noticed a couple of bodies at the back of the shop area. He tried the door – it was locked. Enak nudged him aside and grasped the door handle, giving it both a sharp twist and a push at the same time. A sound of splintering wood accompanied the door falling open and the handle breaking off.

Jason went over to where the two bodies lay. It looked like the woman had been shot by the man, who had then turned the shotgun on himself. Both bore the marks of the disease and had clearly made a suicide pact. Jason covered the bodies with a thin opaque plastic sheet that was tucked under the counter, not so much out of respect but so that Sitara wouldn't have to see what was left of the man's shattered and blood-soaked jaw. She had seen enough horrors recently. He bent down and picked up the shotgun, handing it to Enak, who seemed quite bemused by the weapon. Jason found some boxes of shotgun cartridges on a shelf.

"I know it's probably very primitive to you, seeing as you laughed at the cars, Enak, but it's effective. I'll show you how to use it later."

Jason went into the storeroom and found it still to be well stocked. He called out to the others.

"Come through here. I'm amazed, but there's still food here. Come and help me put some of these boxes in the car. Concentrate on the tinned stuff."

Sitara felt a bit uncomfortable.

"Isn't it stealing? Looting actually?"

"Yes, it is. But it's no good to them, and if we don't take it, somebody else will. It's going to get taken – it may as well be us that gets the benefit."

Sitara knew that Jason was right – looting had become the norm. She'd have to get used to it but, until that time arrived, she just wanted someone else to authorize the theft and appease her conscience. A few minutes later the car was loaded with three boxes containing tins of Heinz Alpha-Getti Pasta, and three other boxes containing Heinz British Style Baked Beans (a catch that particularly pleased Jason). It wasn't particularly nutritious food, but it would do; beggars can't be choosers. They did allow themselves a few luxury items too, picking up toothbrushes, toothpaste, liquid soap, more toilet paper, several more packets of Oreos and some bars of chocolate. A box of Gatorade was also among the booty. As the men loaded the car, Sitara started walking in the direction of the outlet centre. She hadn't forgotten that she needed a change of clothes. There was nothing wrong with what she was wearing, but how could she get the scenes of her nurse's death out of her mind if she was still wearing Suzy's clothes? Jason followed behind her, leaving Enak to look after the car. He walked alongside her.

"You can't just go wandering off on your own. It isn't safe."

Sitara found a shop that had good quality jeans, T-shirts, shirts, and even footwear. Jason kept a lookout while she popped into the fitting rooms with a large bundle of clothes in her arms. She felt a little wicked as she suddenly realized that she had never been into a shop's changing room with more than three items before.

She emerged wearing a pair of black denim jeans, and a white cheesecloth blouse over a white T-shirt. The outfit was complemented by a rather chic pair of cowboy boots. She gave a twirl for Jason and laughed. It was the first time for a while that she had felt like laughing.

"All I need now is a cowboy hat."

Jason helped her stuff extra pairs of jeans and shirts into one of the large customer shopping bags that hadn't been used since the shop staff had evacuated the premises. They were just about to exit the shop when Sitara suddenly stopped by a large wire container.

"Mustn't forget these."

Once she had stuffed some bras and about a dozen pairs of panties into the bag, she was ready to leave. Both were secretly relieved to see Enak still standing by the car, and were about to join him when Sitara spotted a drugstore in the corner of the lot.

"Hang on, Jason. I need to check this out."

Jason watched for a few seconds as Sitara ran over to the drugstore and then sprinted after her. He didn't know what she was after, but he decided that he'd better follow her. Just because the clothes shop had been safe, it didn't mean the drugstore would be. He arrived at the door just as she was coming out of the store. A new plastic bag was stuffed to the brim with tampons, panty-liners, antibiotics and multivitamins. She grinned at Jason.

"They may not be important to you, but they'll be a lifesaver to me. And any other women we meet."

It wasn't long before they arrived at Mechanicsville. It looked pretty much how all towns and cities were looking nowadays; a wasteland of looted and vandalised shops, interspersed with dead bodies. It was hard to believe that such chaos had occurred in such a short time. They passed through the city without stopping, heading out until they reached Route 236 and the St. Mary's County Amish Settlement. It was a long shot but, given the Amish lifestyle and their insular way of life, perhaps the pandemic had passed them by.

A few Amish homes and farms were dotted along the two-lane highway, with several dead-end side roads branching off. It was as they had just passed one of these side roads that Sitara spotted a grey-roofed buggy heading down the track away from them. Jason turned around and drove slowly down the side road to follow it, so as to frighten neither buggy-driver nor horse. The man spotted the car and halted his vehicle, jumping down from his seat to face them.

The buggy driver was in his very early twenties, dressed in the plain practical and traditional clothing that unmistakably identified him as Amish. He was also clean shaven, signifying that he was, as yet, unmarried. He spread his arms wide, not appearing at all frightened by the trio.

"Good day, travellers. How may I help you?"

Jason got out of the car and shook hands with the young man.

"My name is Jason, and the two in the car are Sitara and Enak. We've just come from Bethesda. We were hoping that perhaps we could stay with your community for a few days until we decide what to do next."

The young man looked forlorn and then his smile returned.

"There's not much of a community left now, just myself – I'm Samuel – my father Jacob, my mother Ruth, and my younger sister Miriam. We live on a small farmstead at the end of this lane.

Jason beckoned Sitara and Enak to get out of the car and introduce themselves, and Samuel invited the group to follow him to the farm. Upon arrival, he parked the buggy next to a barn, and Jason did likewise with the car. The three waited outside the house while Samuel went inside to talk to his parents.

A minute later, the rest of the family came outside, Samuel's father stepping forward to shake hands with his visitors. Enak was unsure what this gesture signified but it seemed to be traditional and customary, so he just copied Jason and Sitara. Jacob rubbed his hand a little after retrieving it from Enak's grip.

"We are the Miller family, and you are most welcome to our home and our hospitality. Please come in and take supper with us."

Jason spoke for the group.

"Thank you very much, Mr Miller."

"Please call me Jacob."

"Thank you, Jacob. We don't intend staying too long. Just for a few days until we decide our next move. And I can assure you that we're not infectious. We're all immune."

Jason included Enak in that statement, although, of course, he couldn't be sure that he was telling the truth. In reality, he was making a grand assumption but his gut was telling him that Enak was immune, and his gut had saved him from danger in the past. However irrational it may seem, he trusted his gut now too.

Looking through the car windows, Jacob had a final request before admitting the visitors into the house.

"If you wouldn't mind putting your vehicle in the barn, and leaving the weapons inside it."

The car and guns safely secreted, the group followed Samuel's family into the Millers' home. The house was spacious, as were most Amish homes, a necessity as the Amish often had six or more children. With just the two children, Samuel and Miriam, the Miller family was a little unusual. The interior of the house was painted white and there were no electrical sockets or telephone lines. A wooden perpetual calendar hung on one wall, alongside a banner, upon which were written the Ten Commandments. A beautiful but functional wall clock continued the theme of practical decoration. The living room furniture, rather surprisingly, was upholstered and looked quite comfortable. Sitara was even more surprised to see a refrigerator in the kitchen, believing that the Amish shunned modern conveniences. However, it had been adapted to run on propane gas (which was also the fuel used to light the house at night). A propane gas stove completed the 'mod-cons'.

The bearded but non-moustached Jacob bade everybody sit down.

Jason had noticed many Amish dwellings nearby, but all appeared to be empty.

"If you don't mind me asking, where is everybody else?"

Jacob sighed.

"They are with our Father. For some reason, the Good Lord saw fit to spare my family and me. We knew that the Lord must have saved you too, for if he had not, you too would have perished and joined him by now."

Jacob's wife, Ruth came in from the kitchen with

a tray of coffee and Amish Cinnamon Bread for their guests. Although the bread took about ten days to make, Ruth always liked to have some on hand, and it was a habit that she couldn't break free from, despite the plague having left no one else alive in the community to share it with. She couldn't help staring at Enak, while silently chastising herself for doing so.

"Help yourselves, please. There's plenty more in the kitchen."

Jason took a bite of the bread.

"Mmmm. This really is delicious. Thank you, Ruth."

He waited until he had swallowed the last of his slice, before speaking again.

"As you've kindly offered to let us stay for a few days, perhaps we ought to tell you about ourselves."

Jason had an ulterior motive. The real reason behind his leading the conversation in this direction was that he wanted to know more about Enak, and hoped that this impromptu 'show and tell' would encourage him to open up more about himself.

"As you can probably tell from my accent, I'm from England. I came to the USA a few years ago to work on an engineering project, met a girl, fell in love, and got married. I lost her to the plague. I was with a group of fellow survivors – for some reason the disease appeared to have passed our little community by – but then one day I woke up and everybody else was dead. I couldn't stay there any longer and decided to take my chances on the open road. I was attacked by some other survivors, but

Enak here saved me. We found a car and headed towards your settlement, in the hope that your culture of isolation may have spared you. That's me in a nutshell."

Jacob disapproved of 'found a car' (knowing that it was a euphemism for 'stole a car') but times were unusual, so he gave Jason a free pass on breaking the Lord's eighth Commandment.

Sitara explained that she was a NASA scientist, working on the Voyager Interstellar Mission, and was a Muslim. She told the amazing story of how she had been called to examine a fallen satellite that had been picked up by a factory trawler in the Bering Sea, and how she had been able to identify it as the Voyager One Space Probe, even though the probe was supposedly over 13 billion miles away from Earth and still in communication with NASA. Tears welled up in Sitara's eyes.

"It's my fault. The plague is connected to Voyager One. If we hadn't returned to shore, if the ship had sunk out there, all these people – Jason's wife, your community, all the other people in America, the whole world – they'd all still be alive."

Ruth went over to the distraught young woman and put her arm around her shoulders.

"Don't cry, my dear. It's not your fault. You weren't to know. It's all part of the Lord's plan. We cannot know for what reason He allowed us to suffer this tragedy, but He has a good reason. You can be sure of that. And you don't know that it was anything to do with this spaceship."

Samuel and Miriam looked at each other. They had had several conversations about the plague when their parents were not around and didn't entirely agree that this was all part of God's master plan.

Sitara took a sip of coffee to clear her throat and dried her eyes on a handkerchief that Miriam passed her.

"But I do. It was traced back to Dutch Harbor in Alaska. The fishing vessel docked at Dutch Harbor. The crew and I, we were all patient zero."

Jason took hold of her hand.

"But you didn't spread the disease, Sitara. The crew? Probably, but you're immune. It wasn't your fault. Hang on to that thought."

Enak knew that they would expect him to tell them all about himself. He wanted to tell them the truth, but could they handle it? He decided to start telling his story and see how it went. They had to know sometime. It may as well be now.

"Hello. My name is Enak. You may notice that my features are different to yours. I am shorter, but also markedly stronger. There is a reason for this. I do not know if you are ready to hear it yet, but I shall tell it to you."

The others were intrigued. Enak certainly did look different. He looked a bit like a well-groomed caveman.

"Many years ago – about forty thousand years ago – there were two species of human on this planet, your species and mine. We had been put here as part of an experiment, by a far more advanced and superior race of beings, known as the Jah. We co-existed on this planet for a while, but then we Argons, or what you apparently call Neanderthals, were removed and resettled on a different planet, far from your solar system. We continued to evolve and develop until we became what you see before you."

The reactions of those in the room were varied. Jason had heard part of the story before. Well, except the experiment and advanced super-being part. Samuel and Miriam had always wondered about life on other planets (although they had kept it to themselves), while their parents were trying to reconcile this information with their religious beliefs. Sitara immediately switched to scientist mode.

"So you're really an alien?"

"Not really. This planet is my home planet, as it is yours."

"But you're from outer space?"

Sitara couldn't help but ask questions, it was her nature. It wasn't every day you met an extra-terrestrial being. Ruth, on the other hand, suspected that Enak was a product of the work of the Devil.

Her husband took Enak's presence as a sign from God.

"Praise be the Lord, for He is almighty and has shown us His miracle of life."

Enak found the whole scenario amusing.

"What you call God was actually an alien race, with technology even more advanced than ours."

Samuel was fascinated by the revelations, even though it went completely against what he had been taught by his family and the community.

"It could explain the miracles in the Bible, father."

Ruth was having none of it.

"He's a demon, or at the very least possessed by the Devil. He's the Devil incarnate. May the Lord deliver us from this evil spirit."

The children were expecting their father to join their mother in proclaiming Enak a demon but were surprised at his response.

"Ruth, please calm down. Our guest is neither demon nor Devil. His explanation makes sense. The Lord has many children and Enak is simply one of his other children. If he were the Devil, do you think we would still be alive now? God made everything and everyone in the Universe, including these Neanderthal fellas. The Lord works in mysterious ways, but his works always have a reason and that reason must be good. Looks to me like he sent Enak here to help us."

It wasn't exactly the response that Enak was expecting, but it seemed to be a positive step. He stopped his story there, saying that he needed to sleep, hoping that Jason wouldn't realise that sleeping was merely a diversionary tactic when talking some more could become awkward. He was certain that they weren't ready for the rest of his story. Not yet, anyway. He would tell them everything when he was left with no other choice. He was glad that nobody had asked him how he had come to be on planet Earth, as they wouldn't like the answer. In fact, they would be horrified, quite rightly so, and probably want to kill him.

Ruth calmed down and succumbed to the wise words of her husband. She wasn't completely sure that he was right, but she trusted his judgement. After an afternoon of more relaxed conversation, with Enak all the time pretending to be asleep, Ruth entered the room with the evening meal – *Nachtesse* – a product of a busy day of cooking and baking. Before eating, the four Amish lowered their heads and closed their eyes, entering into silent prayer. Sitara took the opportunity to offer her own silent prayer to Allah, apologising in advance for straying from the Ramadan rituals, which she was pretty sure she wouldn't be able to keep to. She would try to fit in a prayer when she woke up but hoped that Allah would understand the unusual circumstances that she found herself in and would forgive her failings. Jason closed his eyes out of respect but, being an atheist, didn't pray. Instead, he used the time to think about the group's next move. Enak just looked around him, thinking how primitive it was to ask favours and offer gratitude to the Jah, who had obviously been negligent in the care of their charges.

DAY SIXTEEN – 9 MAY

The roar of the motorcycles cut through the silence of the night, heralding their arrival at the Amish farm like a fanfare for the four horsemen of the Apocalypse. Jacob leapt out of bed and grabbed his hunting shotgun, which was stashed away in the kitchen. Visitors were normally welcomed, but nobody who comes calling unannounced at two o'clock in the morning has good intentions. Not these days.

He opened the door to see four Harley Davidson motorcycles lined up facing the door of the house, their exhausts belching smoke like war-horses exhaling warm breath on a cold winter's day. Astride the bikes, which had been stolen from a showroom in Indianapolis the previous day, sat four figures, all dressed in black leather motorcycle gear. They looked fearsome, and the pump action shotguns they held increased that emotion. Jacob stood his ground.

"What do you gentlemen want at this time of the morning?"

The group's leader answered.

"Amish ain't ya? A man of religion?"

Jacob responded, not taking his eye off the man, his hunting rifle pointing at the motorcyclist's chest.

"That I am, praise the Lord. What about it?"

"Well, me and my friends, we're mighty pissed at your god. We wanna know why he saw fit to send this mighty plague to kill our families. Do you have a family, Mister Amish man? I had a family, I had a wife, Carol. I had a daughter, Lynette. I had my best friend, Nolan. Now I ain't got nothing. 'Cept my boy and my new friends here."

Triggs failed to mention that Nolan hadn't died from the plague but that he himself had killed him. And Nolan would never have called Triggs his best friend – as far as he had been concerned, they were just two guys doing a shitty job that nobody else wanted to do. Jacob wasn't interested in Triggs's sob story.

"We've all lost families and friends, sir. And I'll thank you kindly to get off my land and go back to whence you came."

The biker mimicked the farmer.

"Go back to whence I came? Well, ain't you the fancy Dan, Mister Amish man."

Jacob repeated his demand.

"Get off my land."

"Or what old man?"

"Or I won't be responsible for my actions."

The commotion outside had woken Jason, Enak and Sitara, who had been sleeping in the barn. They peeked through a gap in the wood cladding and saw Jacob facing off against four bikers. Jason whispered to Enak,

"Fetch the guns from the car. Old man Jacob's got unwanted company."

Enak took the shotgun and the semi-automatic rifle from the back seat of the vehicle and joined Jason.

Nobody noticed as one of the motorcyclists slipped around the back of the house and entered by the back door. All eyes were on the motorbike group's leader and the Amish farmer. Triggs laughed.

"You're a man of God, old man. You're Amish. It's against your religion to hurt another human being. Y'all ain't gonna hurt me."

The man was right. Jacob used his gun for hunting. He didn't know if he could shoot another human being.

Suddenly the missing biker appeared behind Jacob, holding Ruth and Miriam tightly by their arms.

"Hey, Triggs. Look at what I found. There was a young dude in there too. Took exception to me comin' into the house, but he's sleepin' now."

Triggs took a long look at the two women and wolf-whistled.

"Say Mister Amish man. That's a pair of mighty fine ladies you were hidin' in your house. Mind if we play around a little with 'em? Naw, course you don't. There's only one of y'all and there's four of us. Y'all can watch though. Share the experience."

Jacob was doing his best not to stray from the Lord's teachings, but he wasn't about to let these men rape his wife and daughter either. He glanced up towards the heavens as his trigger finger started to squeeze the shotgun's trigger, slowly, very slowly, as if to give him the chance to change his mind and avoid killing a fellow man.

A shot rang out.

The man-mountain that held Ruth and Miriam prisoner lost his grip on the two women and collapsed like a sack of potatoes, as a mix of flesh, bone, and brain matter gave the two women an unwelcome and nauseating shower.

Panic ensued. The women, covered in remnants of Pete's head, stood gasping in shock as Jacob pushed them back into the house, bolting the door shut. Ruth's motherly instincts came to the fore, and she went to find Samuel and see if he was alright, ignoring the bloody mess that was splattered over her clothing. He was groggy, having been knocked clean unconscious with one punch to the head, but he wasn't seriously hurt. Miriam locked and bolted the back door and returned to her father's side.

Jason was pleased that his shot had turned the situation. He'd picked up a telescopic sight with the rifle when he had raided that sporting goods shop back in Bethesda, and the scope had ensured a clean shot.

Triggs and the two remaining bikers had quickly taken cover behind a large rain barrel beside the house. It didn't afford much protection, and they were forced to huddle together, but it was better than nothing. Triggs called out.

"I don't know who y'all are mister, but as far as I

can see there's still three of us and probably only two of y'all. There's no need for none of us to get hurt. Me and my buddies will just get on our bikes and ride away into the sunset."

Triggs had no intention of leaving quietly. The bikers still outgunned the Amish farmer and whoever was in the barn, even though they were a man down.

"Tell you what, Amish man in the barn…"

Jason called out from his hiding place.

"I'm no Amish man and I won't hesitate to put the next bullet through your head, just like I did your friend's."

Triggs whispered to his colleagues.

"One of you go 'round the back of the house and outflank the dude in the barn. From his accent, I reckon he's a Limey. Prob'ly just a lucky shot that knocked down ol' Pete. They don't usually have guns over there. Probably never shot a gun in his life before today."

Shane, the youngest of the group, started to move. He was enjoying the adventure. School had closed indefinitely, and since he'd joined up with his father, the sixteen-year-old's life had become much more exciting. He silently crept around the back of the building and approached the side of the barn. Suddenly he was looking down the business end of a double-barrelled shotgun, at the other end of which was a fine-looking dark-skinned young woman. He began to calculate the odds of success if he primed his own pump-action weapon, but was stopped in his tracks by a male voice behind him.

"Don't even think about it."

He slowly turned his head to see a short but very stocky man. Enak was unarmed but Shane looked at the size and the strength in the man's forearms and imagined that the man could easily overpower him. He could shoot the man, but then he'd probably be killed by the woman. He was only sixteen and far too young to die. He slowly put his gun on the ground, before being marched inside the barn.

Now Jason's little group had an ace up its sleeve – a hostage. Enak looked over Shane's pump-action shotgun that he had picked up off the ground.

"Primitive but effective, I imagine. Not my weapon of choice though."

Jason called out to the house.

"Jacob? Are you alright in there?"

Jacob watched as his wife put a cold compress on the back of their son's head before shouting back.

"We're all fine. Samuel will have a headache for a few hours, but he'll live."

Jason turned his attention to the two men concealed behind the rain barrel.

"We outnumber you, and now we have a hostage. This scenario can play out one of two ways; we can negotiate your surrender and get on with our business, or we can shoot it out right here and now. While you're considering your options, think on this. We have four guns against your two. You're hiding behind a water butt. You're alive because I'm letting you live. I don't really want to kill you, but I will if I have to. And, don't forget, we have a hostage."

He turned to Shane.

"Say something, lad."

Shane knew what he wanted his father to do.

"Pa, do whatever he wants. He's not joking. Let's just get out of here, while we can."

Triggs knew that he had no choice. He'd lost his wife and daughter; he didn't want to lose his son too.

"OK. We give up. You're in charge."

Jason nodded to his friends, before shouting out his terms for Triggs' peaceful withdrawal.

"Here's what's going to happen. You're both going to unload your weapons and throw the ammunition forward. Then you're going to throw your guns behind you. Then you're going to stand up and walk to the centre of the courtyard, hands in the air. Do you understand?"

Triggs called out that he did.

"Then you'll turn around and start walking back down the approach road. Your bikes will stay here."

"What about my boy?"

Jason turned to Shane.

"What's your dad's name?"

"James Trigger. But everybody calls him Triggs."

The instructions continued.

"Mr Trigger, you'll wait for us two hundred yards before the track meets the main road, wearing nothing but your underwear."

Sitara whispered softly.

"Why have they got to be in their underwear?"

"Because it makes them vulnerable."

"Oh, I see. Good idea."

Jason gave the last of his conditions.

"We'll be leaving here early tomorrow. You'll make yourselves visible when we approach you, we'll pass you, and then - a mile down the road - we'll let your son out of the car. Do you agree?"

Triggs reluctantly agreed although he would have preferred to make a rescue attempt to get his son back.

"Will y'all be turnin' left or right at the main road?"

"That's for us to know and you to find out. Do we have a deal?"

Triggs had no choice.

"We have a deal."

The group in the barn watched as the two men followed the instructions to the letter, before setting off along the side road in the direction of the highway.

Enak kept watch on the dirt road that led away from the farmstead, in case Triggs and his friend decided to do something stupid. When the coast was clear, Jacob let his rescuers back in the house. Jason touched Jacob's shoulder.

"I'm sorry, but you're going to have to come with us. We've got plenty of room."

Jacob protested, echoing Burt Prentice's sentiments, saying that he'd been born in that house and so had his children – it was their home, and it was part of them. Jason understood how he felt, but it was too dangerous for them to stay on their own.

"You're not safe here. What's going to happen

next time some low-life decides to invade your property? You could get killed. Your wife and daughter could be raped. Think of your family."

Ruth intervened, she and Miriam more comfortable now that they had washed the mess off themselves.

"Jacob. The Lord Almighty knows that I want to stay here, but we were lucky tonight. Who knows what might happen next time, when Jason and his friends aren't here. We can't stay here. There's nothing here for us now. Only memories. And we can take our memories with us. The Lord will be with us, wherever we might go. We know that."

Later that same morning, at the crack of dawn, the overladen SUV left the farm, but not before Enak had disabled each of the Harleys, having spent the rest of the night keeping watch in case the two remaining bikers tried to rescue Shane. As the car rumbled along the dirt-track, they could see that Triggs and his accomplice were waiting a couple of hundred yards before the road junction, just as they had been told to do, wearing nothing but their underwear. The SUV turned right and stopped a little over one mile further down the road, where they left their prisoner by the roadside. Free of the extra passenger, the Chevy continued along the road towards Washington D.C.

About ten miles before the capital city, Enak suggested that they stop. The SUV pulled into the next motel and disgorged its passengers. Enak didn't want to say what he had to say out in the parking lot.

It would be better if they were all sitting down.

"We should go inside. I have more to tell you about what lies ahead."

The motel reception area was pleasantly furnished and surprisingly clean, with the furniture perfectly arranged in groups of four chairs around a low-level coffee table. Enak fetched three more chairs over to one of the tables so they could all sit down. Then he went over to a vending machine, ripped the door open, and returned with several bars of chocolate which he tossed into the middle of the table, and seven cans of Dr Pepper which he placed in front of each member of the group. Jason passed around the snacks.

"So, Enak. What do you want to talk to us about?"

Enak took a sip of his drink, enjoying the new taste, but then a serious look came over his face.

"There is something you need to know before we get to the city. You need to be prepared for what you may face in the days to come."

They had a good idea of what they would probably see – hundreds of bodies, in varying states of decay. But there would also be signs of civilisation; it may be mostly empty of living people, but the basic physical infrastructure would probably still be there. They might even find other Immunes, hopefully, more agreeable than the four that had confronted them at the Amish farm. Enak continued.

"I have already told you something of my background, but I am not sure that you really appreciated the enormity of the situation."

Miriam unwrapped a Mars Bar, took a bite and spoke with her mouth a little full.

"You mean that you're from another planet? And that mother called you a demon?"

Ruth blushed, realising that she had misjudged the stranger. He had more than acquitted himself of that charge during the early morning's attack. She felt embarrassed.

"I'm sorry, Enak. I was shocked and startled. It just came out."

Enak smiled.

"You are forgiven, Ruth."

"Thank you, Enak. Your forgiveness is very important to me. And to our Lord."

Enak nodded his acceptance of the apology.

"What I am going to say to you will seem incredible. In fact, you will not want to believe it. It may make you frightened. It should make you frightened. But please do not be scared of me. I am different. It is a long story, but it is important that you know all the facts.

"You can see that I am obviously physically different to you, but yet there are similarities. I am human, but not human like you are. There is a very good reason for this, a reason that will seem both absurd and bizarre to you. You will find it hard to believe, but I assure you that it is true."

Enak looked around the table. His colleagues' eyes were all fixed upon the Argon like cub-scouts gathered around a camp-fire about to hear a ghost story. Enak took a sip of Dr Pepper and continued.

"About forty thousand years ago, you and we - what you like to call Neanderthals - lived side by side. We were subjects of an experiment performed by a far more advanced extra-terrestrial race of beings, the Jah, that involved the manipulation of primate DNA in an effort to create a creature of higher intelligence."

Samuel was hungry and had already started eating a second bar of chocolate.

"When you say 'we' do you mean just your people or ours too?"

"Both species were part of the same experiment."

Ruth felt that she was beginning to understand.

"So these extra-terrestrials were, in fact, the Lord our God."

"Your people gave them various names, I believe."

Sitara interjected.

"Like my god, Allah, who is actually the same god that you worship. Or the Hindu gods, or Zeus, Apollo, Wodin, and so on."

Enak didn't want the conversation to drift into a discussion of what god was the best god or even the true God, or even if gods existed at all.

"Anyway, we Argon were taken off the planet and placed on a different planet many light years away from here. Both humans and Argon continued to develop on their own planets, but we did not fall prey to superstitious beliefs and suffer periods of stagnation. Our technological progress was uninterrupted. This is why we have superior technology."

Sitara was surprised.

"I thought that Neanderthals were supposed to be less intelligent than us, us humans I mean."

"Yes. I notice that your species has this misconception. When we left the planet, we were probably at a similar level of development. But we are far more advanced than you are now - as you will see. Sitara, you are a scientist, yes?"

Sitara nodded.

"Then I think that you will find what I am about to tell you both fascinating and frightening. Please remember that I am not a threat to you and I could do nothing about what has happened. Sitara, you were one of the first people to encounter the spacecraft that you call Voyager One, yes?"

She responded guardedly.

"Yes, I was."

"Did it seem odd to you that, at the same time as Voyager One was on Earth, it was also outside your solar system?"

"Of course it did. It's impossible. We don't have the technology."

"But we do."

"How? How did you do it?"

Jason was more interested in getting to the end of the briefing and didn't want to get side-tracked by a scientific discussion that would leave him and the other four floundering.

"Perhaps Enak can explain the details to you at another time, Sitara. He has more important things to tell us first."

Enak nodded.

"Agreed. It is more important that you know why Voyager One returned to Earth than how. Again, I ask you to not judge me for the actions of my species. I do not agree with their actions."

Jacob took Ruth's hand and squeezed it tightly. What he was listening to didn't tie in with his beliefs, but he found himself engulfed by curiosity. These were most certainly not normal times and he wanted to know everything possible about this new world in which they now found themselves. Enak took another sip of Dr Pepper.

"This drink is very pleasant. I like it."

He paused before continuing

"Anyway, to us, Voyager One was a container, a vessel to transport a deadly virus to your planet. Our planet has become overcrowded and we need to colonise others. We stumbled upon your space probe and it was like – to use your terminology – a gift. No modifications to the planet would be necessary. The spacecraft Voyager One carried a very primitive disc containing information about your planet, and our historians soon realized that it had originated from the very same planet from which we had been forcibly exiled forty thousand years previously. We knew that the atmosphere and gravity would be acceptable to our bodies."

Jason needed clarification.

"So what you're telling us is that this pandemic is an act of biological warfare?"

Enak looked down, his serious face being replaced by one of deep sadness.

"I am ashamed to say that this is true."

"But why?"

"You were in the way. An inconvenience. The Argons have no desire to share the planet."

Jason had served in the British military, he was an ex-Parachute Regiment Captain and was trained in the skills of conventional warfare, but biological warfare was a completely different kettle of fish. Just as conventional warfare uses airstrikes to soften up targets, the invaders had used an organic weapon of mass destruction to soften up planet Earth.

None of the group knew how they should react. They felt anger, a lot of anger, but to rain that anger upon Enak seemed wrong. He had already said that he was different from others of his species, and his actions seemed to support that statement. He hadn't needed to tell them about this. He could have said nothing and allowed them to walk into danger like lambs to the slaughter. Sitara wanted to know more about the disease.

"How did you know that the disease would work?"

"A stroke of luck, or misfortune, depending on your viewpoint. There was a small sample of blood embedded on the inside of one of the panels of the spacecraft. Add to that, the disc attached to the side of the space vehicle contained two images of your DNA structure. It was a simple task for my people to duplicate the DNA and create a targeted virus in our laboratories."

Samuel wanted to know more.

"If it's the perfect virus, then why are we alive?"

"Do you know your blood type?"

"Yes. B negative. Like the rest of my family."

"Sitara, what's yours?"

"B negative."

"Jason?"

"B negative."

"There is your answer. The virus is ineffective on people with B negative blood type."

Jason wondered how the scientists hadn't come up with the answer before, it didn't seem that obscure a reason for immunity, but the disease had had an incubation period of seven days during which both infected and immune showed no symptoms whatsoever. The speed with which the plague had spread, coupled with the collapsing infrastructure, had left research resources severely limited. Identifying enough Immunes in time had been impossible, and Sitara had been their best hope. He was becoming impatient for answers to more pressing questions.

"Forget about the blood types. We're here. We're alive. That's what matters. What I want to know is, how many of you are here – and why aren't you with them?"

"There are several groups of us dispersed all over the planet. And, yes. I was a member of one of those groups."

"So you're the enemy."

"I am what you would call a deserter. I am now an enemy of my own people, what you would also call a traitor. But sometimes you have to support the side that is right, not just the side that shares your ethnicity, culture, or history. I may well be seen as being on the wrong side in the eyes of my people, but I am sure that in your history I shall be seen as choosing the right side. And I am content with my decision. I do not believe in what my people are doing. I believe in the concept of what you call humanity. We can find another planet to colonise, another planet that is devoid of intelligent life. Or a planet that can be modified. We have the technology. Taking your planet is simply the easiest way to solve a problem. This planet seems more attractive, due to our history, but we do not need to be here. I want to help those of you who are still alive take back your planet before the main invasion force arrives."

After what had happened back at the farm in Mechanicsville, the group decided that it would be best to have someone on lookout duty during the night. The entire group had benefitted from Enak's presence, none more so than Jason, who owed the alien his life. Jason, Enak, Samuel, and Jacob were to keep watch during two-hour shifts, although Sitara insisted upon taking Jacob's shift so that he could get a full eight hours sleep and keep his wife company. Besides, she could keep watch just as well as any man could.

Enak took the first shift and was looking down

the road when he heard a noise behind him. His hand moved towards the trigger of Jacob's hunting shotgun which was resting on his lap. A female voice put his mind at ease.

"It's alright, Enak. It's only me, Sitara."

She settled herself alongside the Argon and looked up at the stars. Was Voyager One up there, still travelling through interstellar space, exploring the unchartered heavens?

"Is it still there?"

"Is what still there?"

"Voyager One. Is it exploring space?"

"I doubt it. Not now."

"But it was, wasn't it?"

"Yes, it was."

"At the same time as it was back here on Earth?"

"Yes."

"How did that work?"

"You do not need to know. It's very complicated."

"Enak. I'm a NASA scientist. I get – I got – paid for understanding complicated. It's what I do. And I think I deserve an explanation."

"Shouldn't you be sleeping?"

"I couldn't sleep. Not without knowing how Voyager One could be in two places at once. You've told us why it was here on Earth, but not how. I don't know if I'll ever sleep again if I don't know how. Call it my natural scientific curiosity."

Enak didn't want to be the cause of her never sleeping again and reluctantly began to tell her how the phenomenon had occurred. It felt like explaining a law of physics to a young child, but he understood the reason why she had to know – he was a kindred spirit. He was a scientific historian, whose job was to use his knowledge of primitive technology in order to get certain infrastructures functioning as a temporary measure until more advanced equipment could either be constructed or brought from his home planet. So he decided to grant Sitara's wish, to a small extent at least.

"Has your species succeeded in manipulating subatomic particles yet?"

"We've made a start, yes. Photons and electrons have been manipulated to be in two locations at the same time. I seem to recall that a glass sphere, 40 nanometres in diameter, was forced into a quantum superposition using a laser."

Enak allowed himself a silent chuckle at the pride that the human scientific community held in its ability to perform rudimentary simple quantum tasks, but he felt that he should try to encourage the humans' efforts.

"And how about coupling electromagnetic and gravitational forces? Can you harness and manipulate gravity yet?"

"That's impossible, isn't it? I don't know if anyone is even studying that kind of thing at the moment."

"You are trapped in this small part of your solar system until you do. Interstellar space travel will remain a dream for you until you understand the essence of gravity and can manipulate it. I do not even know if your planet possesses the materials capable of creating the necessary current density that is required to create the kind of engine that powers our spacecraft. Perhaps you will never break free of your cosmic neighbourhood. But you've started to make progress with quantum mechanics – that is a good start."

It seemed a little like a back-handed compliment, but Sitara was grateful for any shred of information that Enak was willing to give her. Not that there was much that she could do with it – NASA and organised scientific research no longer existed. Enak continued.

"But you have a long way to go."

Sitara was hooked and wanted to know more.

"You're saying that Argons have managed to superposition larger objects?"

"You have seen the Voyager craft yourself. You have seen the evidence."

"So Voyager One was simultaneously billions of kilometres away from Earth? We thought one of them must be false. At first, we thought that the one on Earth was fake, but – "

"Both were the same object."

"So how did you do it?"

"Are you sure that your time would not be better spent trying to sleep?"

"Please, Enak. I need to know."

"Very well. I will explain it as simply as I can. Primarily, the environment surrounding the object must meet specific criteria, namely, the object must be in a vacuum and very cold. And what better vacuum is there than outer space?"

This seemed logical to Sitara. Research on Earth bore these facts out.

"So what else needs to happen?"

Enak knew that he was about to leave the scope of mankind's current understanding of quantum mechanics.

"It will be pointless going into great detail. It is something that cannot be explained sitting by the side of a road outside a motel. But I will give you something to think about."

"But I want to know."

"Your species is not sufficiently advanced to comprehend the processes fully."

Sitara was disappointed. Enak picked up a small stone and placed it on the upturned palm of his hand. He turned his hand over and the stone dropped to the ground. He looked at Sitara.

"That is your problem."

Sitara understood immediately what he was demonstrating.

"Gravity?"

"Gravity. The pull of gravity must be overcome. Even at a subatomic level, gravitational forces are trying to create order. You need to control and manipulate gravity. This is why we do not need wheels on our vehicles. The whole process also requires immense amounts of energy. Fortunately, we have access to boundless amounts of energy. You do not."

"Can you tell me more about that?"

"I could, but I will not. It would be like allowing a baby to play with a grenade. At the moment, you would destroy the entire planet. I can tell you no more. Just know that gravity and the ability to manipulate it is the key."

"May I ask you one last question?"

"You may."

"Why did you remove the antennae and other parts?"

"To cut down on the energy required. That is all. We needed only the main body of the vehicle for our plan to be a success. That and your curiosity."

Sitara went back to bed, falling into a deep sleep until it was her turn to keep watch. Her curiosity had been sufficiently satisfied for one night's sleep at least.

The rest of that night was peaceful. The bikers from were in no position follow them, their bikes having been made useless, and nobody else came near the motel. Apart from taking a breather and collecting their thoughts, Enak had another reason to wait before entering Washington DC – he knew what would be certainly be waiting there for them.

DAY SEVENTEEN – 10 MAY

After breakfast, Enak took Jason aside for a private word. The whole group had a right to know what they were letting themselves in for, but he wanted to talk to Jason first. With Jason's support, they could hopefully avoid a confrontation with the other Argons until it became absolutely necessary. Simply surviving wasn't an option – if something wasn't done soon, the main invasion force would arrive and then the remaining vestiges of humanity would be wiped out or enslaved.

Enak and Jason sat down in the motel office to chat, although the word 'chat' seemed too trivial for the conversation that was about to take place. They knew that the others wouldn't interrupt them – Enak and Jason were the main reason why they were still alive, and nobody wanted to upset the balance of the group. Enak had requested the meeting, so he got the ball rolling.

"Jason, there are certain additional things that you need to know about the Argon."

Jason knew the importance of reliable intel. Any information that Enak could give him was important.

"Go ahead, my friend."

"After such a long time away, I do not believe that we have a legitimate claim to Earth. I came here as part of an advance force, to pave the way for an invasion and the colonisation of your planet. I am a scientific historian. My people are unlike any people you have met before. They are completely ruthless and will stop at nothing to get what they want."

Jason knew the type.

"We've had plenty of people like that in our history. Adolf Hitler, Stalin, Pol Pot."

"I have no idea who those people are, but I am talking about a species with absolutely no empathy. An entire race of beings. Empathy has been bred out of my people."

"But you seem like a good person."

"If they knew about my empathy, I would be considered deficient by my own people. I have spent my life hiding my empathy from Argon society. If they knew that I had compassion, I would be considered broken, something to be repaired or destroyed. Thankfully, I am not the only one. There are others. I know of three others that arrived with my part of the vanguard force. There are others hiding in plain sight, embedded in other units. I left in an effort to meet members of your species and help you resist the invasion."

"Do you intend to try to meet up with these other three Argons?"

"If possible. We are working on a solution that may save your people. There is nothing we can do about those that have already died, but the survivors may have a future. It is by no means certain of success, but I am sure that you would prefer that we at least try."

"But if the Argons are as advanced as you say they are, how can we defeat them? And your people are physically much stronger than ours – I saw how you pushed over that heavy racking back in the warehouse."

"We scientific historians do not only study past technology – our technological evolution, although more rapid, mirrored that of your own – but we also do our own private research. We believe we have discovered a way to make our people feel empathy once more. Our victory relies not upon strength, or even numbers, but guile. But, saying that, we need to be prepared for any eventuality."

The two went back to the reception area and rejoined the group, who were chatting amongst themselves. Jason attracted their attention.

"Can we have quiet, please? I have some important information. Enak has told us about his people and their intentions. We are now faced with a dilemma, which is whether we should resist this alien invasion or whether we should accept the situation and try to survive by keeping our heads down and hoping that we don't get noticed. But this has to be a personal decision. I know that you see me as the leader of this little band of misfits – and I'm honoured – but this is something I can't decide for you. You have to make your own decision.

"Enak has told me that the Argons, as a species, have no compassion or empathy. Of course, there are exceptions – Enak is one – but, as a rule, they value your lives no more than we value the life of a cockroach."

Sitara looked at Enak and back again at Jason.

"So, what you're saying is that Earth is being invaded by a race of psychopathic killers?"

"You could say that, yes. I just wanted you all to know the nature of our enemy before you make a decision either way."

Jacob raised his hand.

"May I take a few minutes to discuss it with my family, Jason? For us, any decision needs to be as a unit."

Ruth shook her head.

"That won't be necessary. Jacob's the head of the family. We'll do what he decides. He knows best."

Jacob took his wife's hand.

"I can't make this decision for the family this time, Ruth. Whatever we do, it will be dangerous. Either way, if I make a decision for the family as a whole, I could be sentencing you to death. No, this has to be an individual choice. Stay and fight or become fugitives."

Miriam had had a lifetime of doing what her parents had told her to do and was unsure as to how to react. She didn't know what her father wanted her to do. But she knew that she would feel safer if she stayed with Jason and Enak. She grasped her newfound freedom of choice with both hands.

"I'm going to stay. This is our planet, our home. We had to leave our farm but I'm not going to let them take our planet without a fight."

The rest of her family looked at her, stunned. They weren't used to seeing the mouse roar. But this was what Jacob had really wanted, to be relieved of the onus of deciding things for his family for once. Samuel put his arm around his sister.

"So am I. I wasn't much help back at the farm..."

Ruth stopped him in his tracks.

"Don't say what I think you're going to say, Samuel Miller. You couldn't have done more than you did, and you still have the bump on your head to prove it."

Suitably admonished, Samuel continued.

"...I want to fight too. We can't give in."

Jacob looked at his wife.

"Ruth?"

"Well, Jacob. I would have agreed to whatever you decided, you know that, but – since you've told us we have to make up our own minds this time – I agree with the children. We saw our community destroyed by these evil people, we saw friends and family die in the most horrible way, and someone must stand up to these creatures, someone must punish them. And besides, God is on our side."

Given the new information, Jacob wasn't entirely sure that God was indeed on their side, but he was pleased that his family had decided to stay and fight the Argon. It was his choice too, but saying it out loud was easier with the knowledge that his family agreed with him.

"So that's it, Jason. You're stuck with us. The Miller family will fight."

Sitara had experienced the fear of thinking that she was helpless and all alone when she had been trapped in the isolation room at the hospital. She didn't want to go through anything like that again.

"I'm not going anywhere. I mean, not without

you. A family isn't formed by blood alone. You're my family now. We're family. Wherever you go, I go."

There was no point in asking Enak what he wanted to do. He had already made his allegiance perfectly clear. Jason picked up his rifle.

"I suggest everybody gets their stuff packed up into backpacks, especially food – energy bars and the like – and be ready to move out in thirty minutes. Lock and load your weapons. We don't know what we're going to come up against out there."

Samuel's brow furrowed.

"Why backpacks, Jason? We've got a big SUV."

"Because I'm pretty sure it'll be impossible to drive all the way to our destination. We haven't seen any Argons yet…"

He glanced at Enak.

"…present company excepted, but they're out there and if we stay on the road too long, in a car, we'll be sitting ducks."

Jacob asked the question that was on everybody's minds.

"What is our destination then, Jason?"

"We're going to the White House."

"The White House? Why? What could be at the White House that would interest us? The Government no longer exists. And they're probably all dead by now anyway."

"A small percentage of the population is likely to have survived. Of the whole country maybe six and a half million people. Six and a half million people who are type B negative. Of the population of DC, that means about thirteen and a half thousand people could still be out there somewhere. People who may have banded into small groups, like us. We need to find them and unite them. We're not going to be able to beat the Argons alone. We're not the Magnificent Seven."

Miriam still didn't understand.

"But why the White House?"

"Because it's prepared for a situation like this. Admittedly, the Government was thinking more of being able to deal with a nuclear strike, but it'll have its own communications network, its own power. Maybe we can communicate with people like us in other cities. The State capitals must have similar setups."

The group had decided to stay with Jason, so they didn't question the plan. They didn't have any better suggestions anyway. At least now they had a destination – that had to be better than wandering around aimlessly.

Samuel went over to the vending machine and scooped twenty cereal bars into a plastic bag, while Jason slung his rifle over his shoulder, leaving his hands free to carry two large bottles of water over to the car. Samuel didn't particularly like cereal bars, but he figured that it made sense to take them rather than more chocolate bars. Those that they had eaten the previous night were more of a luxury, a reward for the group having survived the attack at the farmstead, but now they had to be practical. Plus, cereal bars wouldn't melt in the backpacks.

Jason looked at the SUV, and then across the motel parking lot, where he saw three parked cars. He walked over to them and checked under the wheel wells to see if the drivers had left a key anywhere. Two of the cars were secure, but the third had a key tucked in behind the front nearside tyre. Lady luck was smiling on them again. He checked inside the car before returning to the group and handing something to Sitara.

"Please tell me you know how to drive."

Sitara looked at the key in her hand.

"Yes. I can drive."

"Manual? I mean stick-shift?"

"Yes."

"The SUV is cramped. You and Enak can follow behind in the car."

"Which one?"

"The blue one on the end."

"The Mustang?"

"Yep. It's thirsty, but it's got a full tank of fuel and we're not going much further."

Sitara was excited. She'd always wanted to drive a Ford Mustang. She knew it would only be for a few miles, but that didn't matter to her.

Exactly forty-two minutes later the SUV and the Mustang pulled up outside the Southern Avenue Metro station. A strange atmosphere permeated the city, the wide avenues deserted, devoid of the normal daily commotion of commuters trying to get to their workplaces on time. They had half expected to see abandoned cars strewn all over the roads – dozens of doomsday movies and TV series had primed them for that spectacle – but the roads were almost empty. Here and there was a decaying corpse, but those were the exception, not the rule. Sitara was glad that there seemed to be fewer dead on the streets than in Bethesda, she never wanted to see so many dead people again.

Jason opened his driver's door and got out of the car, scanning his surroundings for signs of life. He went round to the back of the SUV and opened the tailgate, reaching inside for his backpack. Sitara and Enak got out of the Mustang and joined him, as he addressed the rest of the group.

"This is the end of the line, folks. Time to stretch our legs. We're going to walk the rest of the way."

The rest of the group obediently took their backpacks out of the vehicles and followed Jason over to the entrance of the Metro station, feeling naked and vulnerable now that they were abandoning the cars. A supermarket flyer lay on the paving outside the station entrance, serving no purpose now but to create an aesthetic distraction to the stillness of the scene. Ruth glanced up at the post by the entrance, which identified the location by its white capital M subscribed by a horizontal green bar. The words Southern Avenue Station were written on the vertical axis of the post, each individual letter tipped 90 degrees on its side. Ruth had never seen words written in that style before. She had never ridden in a metro train before, nor any train in fact, but she wasn't going to be able to do that now either. A functioning public transit system was something that they wouldn't see again for a long time, if at all. She was the last one to cross the drab grey paving slabs outside the station, pass through the open vertically barred gates, and onto the reddish-coloured brick-style flooring of the station's entrance hall.

As they descended the dead escalator to the platform, a little light rain started to fall, so they headed straight for one of the shelters that stood in the centre of the platform. Once out of the drizzle, Jason explained what the plan was.

"We're going to travel underground from here, through the tunnels. It'll be pitch black, so we'll walk in single file, myself at the front and Enak at the rear."

Enak had a suggestion.

"Would it not be better if I were in front? If there are any Argon patrols in there, they will see me first and the few seconds that we may gain before they realise that we are hostiles may prove to be valuable."

Jason nodded agreement to the Argon's suggestion.

"Enak is right. He'll go point and I'll take the rear. Could somebody give Enak a flashlight?"

Miriam went to pass Enak a flashlight, but he waved a finger.

"It is ok. I don't need one. My eyesight is very good in the dark. We evolved excellent night vision in our early days on Argonorian 3."

Samuel liked the sound of that.

"Cool, dude."

His mother looked at him, having never heard those words come out of his mouth before. She was going to say something but didn't, realising that he must have picked up this strange term while on rumspringa, the period that Amish adolescents spend away from the community experiencing all the virtues and vices of the outside world.

Enak gestured to the other six to wait a few seconds. He walked over to where a metal pipe lay on the platform and picked it up. Approaching the edge of the platform he deftly tossed the tube so that it straddled the second and third rails. Nothing happened. Jason nodded his head.

"The tracks have no power, but we should still keep our distance from the third rail. For safety reasons. The power could come back on at any time."

The rest of the group knew that this was unlikely, as the city's power grid had been shut off – probably by the Argons – but it was better to be safe than sorry. They climbed down from the platform onto the tracks, Ruth with a little assistance from her husband. She wasn't used to climbing around and over things, as there had been no call for it on the farm. Her husband had done that kind of stuff and, if he ever needed help, the rest of the community had been only too willing to give a helping hand. But she was quite enjoying this adventure. She was seeing things and doing things that she had never experienced before. It was like a potentially deadly adventure holiday. It was dangerous, but with Jason and Enak to guide her and God by her side, she now felt quite relaxed about the enterprise.

The rain started falling harder as they approached the entrance of the tunnel. Normally, they would have seen a concrete tube, sparsely lit by the lamps that were lined up at regular intervals along the walls. They would have perhaps seen the lights and heard the whine of an approaching or disappearing train. But all they saw was a dark abyss. Suddenly the tunnel was dimly illuminated as Jason switched on his flashlight.

"You may have the eyesight of a cat, Enak, but we don't. We'll feel better seeing where we're going."

Enak nodded and this time accepted the offer of Miriam's flashlight, switching it on and allowing its beam to reach into the darkness.

The seven advanced, keeping well away from the third rail, each of them occasionally looking behind them as daylight gradually disappeared from view. Ruth tightened her grip on her husband's hand. She had never been in a situation like this before, being used to the open spaces of the farm and the Amish community. Now wasn't the best time to discover that she was claustrophobic, but she trusted in God to help her through this ordeal.

Very soon any remaining illumination had disappeared and the only light they had was from the flashlights, making everyone except Enak a little more nervous. They edged their way slowly along the tunnel, placing all their faith in the Argon and Jason to keep them out of trouble, Ruth holding Jacob's hand and Miriam holding her brother Samuel's hand.

All four of them felt a need for both human and family contact to calm their nerves. Sitara would have loved to hold Jason's hand – for security purposes of course – but he couldn't afford to be distracted from protecting their rear, so she gritted her teeth and walked steadily along the tunnels, masking her fear with fake bravado. Jason sidled up behind her and whispered in a hushed tone low enough that the others couldn't hear.

"It's ok to be nervous. I'm nervous too. But I'm right behind you. I won't let anything happen to you – to us."

This made Sitara feel a little better, although she was disappointed that he had noticed just how nervous she was. She thought she had been hiding it quite well.

Each time they approached a station - Congress Heights, Anacostia, Navy Yard, and Waterfront – brought a new risk. Of course, they were walking into the unknown with every step between stations too, but as the tunnel opened up to reveal each station, it also opened up the possibilities of an ambush. Having successfully negotiated their way past the four stations, their next destination was L'Enfant Plaza, a major subway intersection where they would have to change tunnels and follow either the Orange Line or the Silver Line to McPherson Square. They would then have to walk the rest of the route to The White House above ground.

As they neared L'Enfant Plaza, Enak suddenly raised his hand and put a finger of his other hand to his lips. The group following him waited silently as he whispered.

"Stay here. I am sure I just saw a narrow beam of light crossing our path, at about knee height. We have to be careful not to disturb it. It could be a trap or, at best, it could set off an alarm."

Enak moved forward and very deliberately stepped over an invisible obstacle. He waved Jacob forward.

"I am going to guide your leg over the light beam."

Jacob looked at where Enak was pointing to but saw nothing.

"What light beam Enak? I can't see anything."

"You cannot see it, but I assure you that it is there. The light frequency is outside of your spectrum of visibility. I apologise in advance for the physical contact, but there is no other choice."

Enak put one hand underneath the man's thigh, while Jacob placed a hand on Enak's shoulder.

"Jacob, when you feel the pressure of my hand lifting your leg, raise your other leg towards your chest and I will lift you up, turn and place you on this side of the obstacle. Do you understand?"

"Yes. I understand, Enak. Pressure. Lift the other leg. Got it."

With one swift movement, Jacob was on the other side of the light beam. Jacob was impressed.

"Praise the Lord, you really are strong. You picked me up as if I were a child."

Samuel was next, and the operation was

executed with similar ease and precision. Then it was the turn of Miriam. She was both nervous and a little excited by what was about to happen. Enak apologized in advance and placed his right hand under her left thigh. She gave a gasp and put her left hand on the Argon's right shoulder. She was lifted in the air in a motion that made her feel like a ballerina, before gently landing on the other side of the beam.

Only Ruth and Jason remained. Ruth walked forward and prepared to be lifted over the obstruction. She looked at Jacob as Enak explained what he was going to do, and her husband nodded to her that it was going to be alright. The Argon placed his hand under her thigh and started to lift her, just as he had all the others, but suddenly she wriggled free.

"I'm sorry, I'm sorry, I'm sorry. But only my husband has touched me there."

Jason rushed forward and led her to the other side of the beam, knowing that there was no point in holding back now – the beam was already broken. The important thing was to be prepared for anything that might happen next.

The silence was profound as they waited in the darkness, their flashlights switched off. They couldn't even see their hands in front of their faces. They heard whispers from the darkness, but far too quiet to make out what they were saying. Was it English or some other strange alien language? He had no idea what the natural language of the Argon sounded like, but Jason was certain that he'd be able to recognise a human tongue. Suddenly they were blinded by the glare of a trio of flashlights. A voice punctured the silence.

"Put down your weapons and identify yourselves."

The dazzling light was moved slightly away from the group's eyes, allowing the seven to at least make a semblance of seeing who was blocking their path, even if they were only silhouettes. The voice repeated its order.

"This is Gunnery Sergeant Lavisser, of the 1st Battalion, 10th United States Marine Corps. Identify yourselves and put down your weapons."

Jason motioned to the others to do as they were told.

"My name is Jason, Jason Green. We're a small group of survivors, trying to make our way to the White House, the PEOC room."

"Why would you want to go there?"

"We were hoping we might make contact with other groups of survivors, here in Washington D.C. or maybe even in other states."

"I can tell you now, Mr Green, there's no point in trying to get to the White House. It's in enemy hands."

Sergeant Lavisser noticed Enak at the back of the group, trying to look as inconspicuous as a five-foot six-inch stocky Argon could.

"Is that an Argon you have there?"

Jason was surprised to hear the Gunnery Sergeant call Enak's species by name.

"It is."

"Prisoner or friendly?"

"He's with us, he's a friend."

"Mr Argon, would you mind stepping to the front of your group please, so that I might take a better look at you?"

Enak made his way to the front. A voice called out from the darkness.

"Alemal. It is Enak! It is Enak!"

A female Argon moved into the light.

"*Ej, in ilewk, Enak?*"

"*Oidn, in ilewk imim, Alemal.*"

The sergeant gave a diplomatic cough.

"Please, guys. We humans don't have those translator gizmos that you Argon folks have."

Enak put his hand out to shake Sergeant Lavisser's hand.

"Of course. I am sorry. It is just that we did not know if the other were still alive."

"No problem, Mr Enak. We have Miss Alemal, Miss Siroll, and back at base we have a guy named Eled."

Jason's ears pricked up.

"Base? Is there an organized resistance?"

The sergeant shook his head.

"I wish there was. But we're just a band of survivors who kinda stumbled into each other, just like you. One of our guys was a secret service agent in the White House, and he knew about a secret bolt-hole down here in the tunnels."

"How many of you are there:"

"Fifteen Marines, two doctors, three nurses, a

lawyer – not that we have any need for his professional services – two short order cooks, and a couple of families. Plus the secret service guy. Plus the three Argons of course."

The sergeant led the seven newcomers away from the tracks along a hidden pedestrian tunnel until they arrived at a large steel door. He rapped on the door in a pre-agreed rhythm and the door swung open just enough to let the returning group pass through it. Sitara was surprised – as was the rest of the group – at what she saw before her. Sergeant Lavisser could see that they were impressed.

"This is a replica of the POEC room at the White House, all the way down to the finest detail. So our secret service agent tells us anyway. I've never seen the original. The furniture, comms, and everything else up there has been duplicated down here. We have electricity, thanks to a couple of generators, but we don't have comms with the outside world. I don't know if that's a good thing or a bad thing. Probably a good thing. If we could transmit to the outside world – what's left of it – the Argon could maybe hone in on our signal. As for food, we've enough food and water down here to last a couple of years. Anyway, take a look around and make yourselves at home."

For the first time since the plague had broken out, the group felt normal again and the holocaust that they had witnessed seemed to belong to another world. Tucked safely within the walls of this hidden lair, it was almost possible for them to forget that, outside, humanity was facing a threat to its existence such as it had never confronted before.

DAY EIGHTEEN – 11 MAY

Jason stared with disbelieving eyes at the scene of devastation before him. It was hard to believe that such carnage could have happened in so short a time. Torn limbs and mutilated bodies were everywhere, testimony to the superior physical strength of the Argons.

Sitara clung on to him, fearful that the immediate danger hadn't yet gone. She felt a need to hold a fellow human being, a need for the warmth of a human body not only to protect her but to remind her that she was still alive. Jason, in turn, responded by holding her even tighter, confirming his own survival. Everybody needs a hug sometimes.

The room had become eerily silent after the chaos that had enveloped it just a few minutes earlier. Tears were trickling down cheeks, but nobody was audibly sobbing. All they could do was look around and thank their particular gods – if they had any – that they were still alive.

A Marine picked his way through the dead bodies and pointed his Heckler and Koch HK M27 automatic rifle accusingly at Jason.

"Your Argon did this. We had no trouble until you came here. It's a helluva coincidence that you turn up and we get attacked. We've been safe here, but you turn up with your Argon friend and all hell breaks loose."

It had been a bloodbath. The large boardroom table was on its side and the chairs that had once been placed tidily around it were strewn all over the place, many of them broken, mirroring the broken bodies of their fallen friends and colleagues.

Jason just stood there, saying nothing, casting his mind back to the bloodbath that they had just experienced. The humans had fought valiantly but had been thrown around the room like rag dolls. Skulls had been crushed and limbs ripped from bodies as if an angry child in a tantrum had taken his bad mood out on its dolls. But these had been living, breathing human beings who were now just a pile of random body parts strewn haphazardly around the room. There was truth in what the marine was saying, someone had led the Argon warriors to the hideout, but he didn't believe for one second that Enak was the traitor. Rather than simply relive the battle, he concentrated upon the role that each Argon had played in the melee.

He glanced over at the crumpled bodies of the Amish couple, Jacob and Ruth, entwined together in a tragic lovers' death-knot. Ruth had known that she and her husband were about to die, calling out to her creator for mercy. Jason wasn't a religious man – far from it – but he would never forget how her faith had been strong to the very end, imploring her god for mercy with the words *Dear Holy Father, have mercy on us, just as a loving father has mercy on his children*. He respected her strength of belief even though he didn't share it.

Jacob had tried to protect his wife from the ravages of the Argon attackers, attempting to protect her with his own body, but he had paid the ultimate price. His head had been almost severed from his torso, a vice-like grip twisting it free from his body before a similar punishment was meted out to Ruth. They looked peaceful enough now, although their deaths had been anything but.

Jason had tried to save them but had been pulled away at the last minute by Enak, as a huge Argon fist was about to piledrive its way through the Brit's skull. The attacking warrior lost his balance and Enak saw his opportunity. He smashed his own fist into the Argon's chest, shattering the ribcage and driving shards of bone directly into his adversary's heart, killing him instantly.

He remembered seeing Eled scoop up a young six-year-old girl, Jasmine, and literally hurl her across the room to her father, just before an Argon warrior could stamp on her. Eled then squared up directly to the Argon, allowing the father and daughter enough time to run into an ante-room where they would be safe – for the moment, anyway. After a terrifying struggle, that personal battle had ended with the enemy Argon pinned down by Eled's knee across his throat, ramming it against his windpipe with all the force that he could muster. Once he was certain that the Argon was dead, Eled staggered to a wall and leaned against it, grimacing with pain. His arm was broken in three places, and he needed a few seconds respite before he launched himself back into battle once more, handicapped by his injury but not allowing it to force him out of the fight.

Siroll had fought like a woman possessed, fighting as a tigress might to protect her cubs. Jason recalled her grabbing two Argon warriors by their necks, smashing their heads together with such force that their skulls exploded in a cloud of blood, brains, and sinew. She then turned her attention to the main entrance of the room where a warrior was about to leave the fight with a screaming and flailing Miriam tucked securely under his arm. Siroll wasted no time and bounded after the Argon as if her life depended upon it. She was under no illusions as to what the man's intentions were and she wasn't going to let that happen while she still had a say in the matter. The Argons were distant cousins of these humans, and their weak points were the same. The Argon sensed somebody coming up behind him and turned to repel an impending attack, loosening his grip on the Amish girl and allowing her to drop to the floor. He bared his teeth at Siroll and lunged forward to engage her in hand-to-hand combat. But Siroll was too quick for him, parrying his attempted blow and reaching between his legs. She clasped a super-strong hand around his testicles and squeezed with all her might until the twin orbs shattered in her hand. The pain was excruciating, and the warrior collapsed in a sobbing heap before Siroll bent down and broke his neck.

Although it seemed that much more time had passed while Jason replayed the battle in his mind, it was, in reality, only a few seconds. He moved in front of Enak, a human shield protecting a friend.

"You're right, mate. I agree that we were betrayed, but it wasn't Enak. I trust him with my life."

The Marine kept his rifle pointed at Enak, although if he fired the weapon now, the bullets would hit Jason rather than the Argon.

"So who did betray us then? It has to be an Argon. No human would betray his own species."

"You need to get out more if you believe that, but I think I know who gave us up."

Jason couldn't remember seeing Alemal in the fray. Of course, the room had been a maelstrom of confusion, but his military training had kicked in and he had become acutely aware of his surroundings and what was going on, even while he himself was fighting the intruders. Enak, Siroll, and Eled had all fought valiantly, but he had no recollection of Alemal even being in the main room of the POEC while the battle was raging. He suddenly had an idea of how to prove his Argon friend's innocence. He turned to Enak.

"May I have your translation device, Enak?"

Enak removed the device from behind his ear, its removal making a slight popping sound as it disconnected from his head. He didn't know exactly what Jason's intention was, but he trusted the ex-paratrooper. Jason placed it on the seat of the only unbroken chair.

"And yours too, Eled, Siroll, Alemal?"

Eled and Siroll removed their devices and placed them alongside that of Enak.

"Alemal? Can you take your translation device out, please?

Alemal glared at the rest of the survivors.

"This is a waste of time. You have got the guilty one. Enak is the traitor."

It was true. In her eyes, Enak was a traitor. He was fighting with the humans against his own people. What greater betrayal could there be than turning on your own blood? She lunged to her right and pulled Miriam in front of her, holding her tightly so that she couldn't escape. She drew her pistol and held it to the poor young woman's head as she edged her way towards the door with her hostage.

"If anybody tries to stop me leaving, I will kill the girl."

The survivors knew that she wasn't bluffing. She was the Argon spy, and that meant that she had no compassion. She wouldn't hesitate to kill Miriam. There was no point in trying to negotiate with her.

Enak's reactions were cat-like. In one swift motion, he drew Jason's sidearm from its holster, aimed it at Alemal's head and fired. Miriam fell to the floor, for the second time that day, as the bullet rocketed through Alemal's eye at such an angle that it obliterated what once had been her brain. The group turned as one, to see a tear trickle down Enak's cheek before he turned away to hide his face from his friends. Siroll picked up the translation devices from the chair, helping Eled to reconnect his – his broken left arm was next to useless – before replacing her own. Sitara, who had moved closer to her, leaned in towards the Argon and whispered.

"Was Enak crying?"

Siroll responded in an equally quiet voice, not wanting to highlight Enak's sorrow at what he had just done.

"Alemal was his *ekm* - what you humans would call his wife. Enak did what was right and necessary – he knows that – but it was at a great personal cost."

Eled had been gritting his teeth, trying to ignore the pain that wracked his damaged arm, but it had become too fierce to bear. The two surviving nurses had noticed the blood starting to drain from his face and rushed over to help him, but he needed better medical care than the POEC room could provide. Siroll crouched alongside the Argon and took an object from her pocket.

"Here, let me help. I have something that can fix this."

The two nurses moved a little away from their patient. Argon and humans were of the same original genus, but it would clearly be better if he were treated by someone who knew the Argon physiognomy. Siroll looked into Eled's eyes.

"You know this is going to hurt, do you not, Eled?"

"Yes, I understand. Please do it. Now. *Azimuuh amak eherehs ay ajnuvuk apufm.*"

Sitara whispered to Enak.

"What did he say?"

Enak looked on, as Siroll checked for the specific locations of the breaks.

"He said that it hurts like the bone-breaking ceremony. *Ajnuvuk apufm* is one of the few rituals that we still maintain from the old days. Nobody believes that it's really necessary, but it seems to be one of the few rites that we have not been able to extricate ourselves from. It is what you might call a coming of age ritual, in which both males and females have all four limbs deliberately broken to show their inner strength. They are then repaired using the tool which Siroll is holding in her hand. We are given the tool after the ceremony and can use it in future if we are injured."

Eled's face screwed up in pain as Siroll placed a pen-like object over the first break. She pressed a button on the shaft of the device and Eled screamed out in pain.

Sitara winced and looked away.

"What is that thing? She's torturing him."

Enak took an identical item from his own pocket and showed it to the scientist.

"We call it an *izimutam ahc obmohc*. It puts the disturbed molecules back to where they should be. And yes, it is very painful."

"How does it work?"

Sitara winced as Eled let out another shriek of

pain.

"It uses electromagnetism to relocate displaced molecules. For example, the molecules of the bones of the arm of Eled have been pushed out of position, causing the break. The tool simply returns those molecules to their original position. It is quite simple really."

"It looks barbaric. It's like a piece of torture equipment."

"As a medical procedure, it is very efficient, but as a superstitious ritual, I agree. It is barbaric. However, Argon society does not appear to possess the communal will to cease the practice. I do not know why. There is no logic to its continuance."

Jason's mind was momentarily distracted as his mind drifted back to the last meeting back at the Square when he and his neighbours had decided to leave their homes in search of fresh supplies, shelter, and safety. He wondered how his life would be now, had that small community survived that night. He'd have been able to share the responsibility of guiding the group with Patrick and Marshall, for sure. But that was a moot point now – they were all dead. His military training had brought his small group thus far, although the best soldiering skills in the world couldn't have prevented the massacre that had just taken place.

He looked at the five surviving Marines who were, in turn, looking at him. Neither Jason nor the soldiers seemed certain of what to do next. They'd lost their sergeant in the battle and, as Privates, now felt like a rudderless ship and could really use some guidance. One of the Marines spoke up,

"I saw you in that fight. Are you ex-military?"

Jason nodded.

"I was a Captain in Number Two PARA; Second Battalion, Parachute Regiment."

The Marine was impressed.

"That was you guys in the Falklands wasn't it?"

"Yes, it was."

The five Marines huddled together in a quiet but important discussion; they respected the reputation of the elite British Army Regiment and came to an agreement. The Marine held out his hand to Jason.

"If you're willing, we'd like you to take charge. We're not long out of boot camp."

Jason didn't particularly want to lead this new larger group, but he could see in the Marines' eyes that that was exactly what they were hoping for. Jason was forced to accept that the role of leader had been thrust upon him once again. Reluctantly, he opened the discussion about their immediate futures.

"This place has been compromised so we know we can't stay here. But we can't just leave and run around like headless chickens. Anybody got any suggestions of where we should go?"

He looked at each of the faces before him in turn.

"Anyone?"

Silence. Jason didn't know if they were still in shock or just felt that they had nothing to offer.

"OK. I think we should find a high vantage point. Is there a very tall building in this city?"

One of the Marines found his voice.

"Skyscrapers aren't allowed in the city, but there are some tall buildings in Arlington. It's about four miles away. The tallest is at 1812 North Moore Street. Not many companies have offices there. Don't know why – it's a nice building."

Jason was interested.

"Is it a good vantage point?"

"Well. As I said, it's tall. Thirty-five stories, five low-rise elevators, five hi-rise elevators, three jump elevators, and two freight elevators. Floor to ceiling windows, 360-degree vision, typical floor size…"

Jason stopped him before he could reel off any more of the building's specifications."

"How do you know all that?"

One of the Marine's colleagues laughed.

"He's a nerd. Obsessed with architecture."

Jason turned back to the nerd-Marine.

"So you think it'll be a good vantage point? I don't want us to be surprised again."

That was the most important thing. Jason had felt a little uneasy about being underground, but he had taken solace in the fact that the hideout was an official government shelter and should have provided top quality protection. He much preferred to be up high, where he could see if anyone approached.

"Anyone else got any suggestions?"

The group murmured amongst themselves, but the consensus was that they had nothing else to suggest.

"Right. We'll head over to this building in

Arlington then. Get your stuff together. Pack only what you can carry, and we'll head out under the cover of darkness."

With the Argons having superior night vision, Jason wasn't sure that moving after dark would make much difference, but at least it should make the rest of the group feel a little more secure – even if it was only an illusion.

The Potomac River was going to cause a problem. Whichever route the group of survivors chose would entail crossing the river, and that brought with it additional risks. If they took the southernmost route, they would have to negotiate the Arlington Memorial Bridge. The northernmost route meant crossing the Francis Scott Key Bridge. The third alternative was to cross via the Theodore Roosevelt Bridge which meant crossing Theodore Roosevelt Island. Crossing a bridge meant there would be no cover once the group were on it. All three possible routes were more or less the same length – about four miles long, so it didn't really make a difference which bridge they used, in terms of time, but the amount of time that they'd be on the bridge would be the deciding factor. Jason turned to the Marine who had suggested moving to 1812 North Moore.

"What's your name, Marine?"

"US Marine Private Tyler Roberts, Sir. But you can call me Geek. Everybody else does. It's kinda a friendly nickname. I like facts and figures."

"Well, Geek. Which route do you think we should

take?"

"I reckon we should cross the river by the Francis Scott Key Bridge, the northernmost. It's the shortest at 1,701 feet. Theodore Roosevelt is nearly twice as long at 3,143 feet in total, and Arlington Memorial is 2,162 feet. Plus when we get to the other side, we'll be closer to 1812 North Moore. Psychologically, that'll be good. I guess."

Fifteen minutes later the group cautiously left their sanctuary, a graveyard of bad memories and broken bodies, and headed along 7th Street SW towards Jefferson Drive SW. Once the area would have been a hive of activity, the museums drawing people in from far and wide, but now it was as deserted as the rest of the city. None of the routes provided much cover, this particular part of DC being a remarkably green and open area, so they were forced to dart between the large buildings in groups of three or four, so as not to compromise the whole group if they were spotted. Once a quartet was safely huddled against the walls of one building, the next small group would make the dash for safety. Each time a group made the sprint from one building to another; twelve other hearts would leap into the mouths of the rest, aware that they could all die at any second.

It was a relief when the group made it to the bridge without incident. There had been so many times when they had been out in the open and could have been attacked, but they arrived at the Francis Scott Key Bridge unscathed. They could see their objective quite clearly, 1812 North Moore Street, but they were now faced with the most dangerous part of their journey. Once they started crossing the bridge they would be particularly vulnerable, especially once they were away from the riverbank.

The bridge itself looked harmless enough, a four-lane highway with modern streetlights and guardrails belying the fact that it was Washington DC's oldest existing bridge across the Potomac River. Before the plague, it would have seen about 62,000 cars per day crossing it, but now it was almost empty, except for a handful of abandoned cars straddling the highway. There was no logical reason for those cars to have been there – death by plague wasn't so sudden that a victim would be caught by surprise while driving across the bridge. Perhaps these cars belonged to people who had no family and their drivers had gone to the bridge to drown themselves in the river. It would explain the large number of bloated and disfigured corpses floating underneath the bridge.

The group scanned the bridge, looking for anything that might be suspicious, although they had no choice but to cross the bridge if they wanted to get to 1812 North Moore. The bridge was too long for them to adopt the same strategy as they had to get past the Smithsonian, the Washington Monument, and along Virginia Avenue. Now they wouldn't be even remotely safe until they were safely ensconced as high up as possible in 1812 North Moore.

Jason looked at the faces of the small band of

survivors. They looked tired from the effort of having survived for so long, exhausted both physically and mentally. They looked scared – but it would be foolish not to be scared. They had all witnessed the carnage at the Metro Station. They wanted this all to be over, they wanted their old lives back. But that would never happen.

Jason gathered the group around him.

"Ok, everybody. I'm not going to lie to you. This is going to be dangerous. But we have no choice. Keep together, in single file, but close to each other. It's a wide bridge but we need to keep to the middle of the road, away from the sides. I think it'll be safer. Are you all up for it?"

The group nodded and Jason gave the order to move out. The bridge looked a lot longer, now that they were about to cross it. Enak went first, followed by the rest, taking an invisible line down the middle of the bridge. The Marines were interspersed with the civilians, as were Eled and Siroll, with Jason bringing up the rear of the column just as he had done in the Metro tunnel.

It was a peaceful day, clear blue skies broken only by the occasional small white cloud breaking the palette. Ahead five cars were bunched together in such a way that the group had to take a small diversion away from the centre of the road. Jason signalled to the group to wait while he and one of the Marines checked that it was safe to continue. Carefully, they approached the vehicles and looked through the car windows to ensure that there were no hidden surprises inside. The passenger areas of the cars were empty. Jason moved to the front of the line and gestured to the nearest Marine.

"We'd better check the boots."

"Why do we need to check our boots?"

"The car boots. The trunks of the cars."

"Ah. Why didn't you say so?"

Jason gave a sigh. There would always be the occasional confusion between British and American speakers of the same language.

The car boots were checked and everything appeared to be okay, so the small band of men, women, and one child started to edge their way past the obstruction, only a couple of feet from the side of the bridge.

Suddenly, confusion reigned as three Argon warriors leapt over the guardrail. Two of them grabbed Sitara and Miriam, each holding one of the women under an arm, as easily as a child might carry a teddy-bear, while the other threw punches at nearby Marines who had instinctively turned to try and prevent the kidnap. It was all over in a flash, and the three aliens threw themselves into the waters of the Potomac, disappearing from view.

The two women were suddenly aware of being dragged underwater. They struggled as best they could, fighting both their captors and the panic that being hauled underwater was provoking. Each woman had a large palm clasped over her mouth, while stubby fingers pinched their noses closed. The Argons were highly efficient swimmers, and the speed at which they swam underwater to a bank further down the river, was the only thing that prevented the women from drowning.

The nine who were left on the bridge were frozen in shock for a moment before they were aware of Jonas shouting at them to run. Samuel was beside himself.

"We can't leave them. We can't leave my sister."

As the others ran to the Arlington side of the bridge, Jason turned and ran back to where the stricken young Amish man was standing. He grabbed Samuel's arm and half-dragged him off the bridge to where the rest of the group was now tucked behind a bush. He held Samuel by the shoulders and looked him in the eye.

"We're not leaving the girls behind, Samuel. Not Miriam. Not Sitara. If they'd meant to kill them, they would have done so. We'll get them back. I promise."

Siroll joined the two men.

"Jason is correct, Samuel. They have been taken, not killed. We will get them back"

Samuel knew that the main reason he and his sister were still alive, was because of Jason and Enak. He trusted the men. If anyone could get the girls back, it was these two guys.

The three Argons and Jason moved a few yards away from the rest of the group and began to prepare a whispered plan. Jason needed to know what they were up against.

"Why did they kidnap the girls instead of killing

them? Or the rest of us, come to that?"

Siroll felt uncomfortable telling Jason of the fate that awaited Miriam and Sitara, but there was no way to sugar-coat it.

"They will be auctioned off and become the sex slave of whoever buys them. Argon women are treated little better, but at least there is an element of choice about whom we spend our lives with. We are allowed two refusals to marry, but if a third man wishes to marry us – we have no choice and become our new husband's property. Captured women don't even have a choice. Eled, Enak, and I are disabled in the eyes of Argon society. We care about others. We have compassion. But remember, we are the exception, not the rule."

Eled continued.

"There is a waiting period of three days while invitations to bid are distributed to the most revered warriors, and the women are examined to determine their menstrual cycles. A menstruating woman is deemed a particularly fine prize, so, if she is approaching the time that she will bleed, the sale is sometimes delayed. I know it does not sound like it, but that's a good thing. If that is the case with either Sitara or Miriam – preferably both – that may give us a little more time."

Jonas shook his head.

"We can't leave them with the Argons for a second longer than we need to."

Enak had an idea.

"I have thought of a way to rescue them, but we

will need help from one of the nurses."

Jason didn't like the sound of that, but Enak continued to explain his plan.

"You have seen how Argon men carry your females under one arm as if they weighed nothing? Do not forget that Eled and I are also Argon. We possess the same strength. If we can get to where the women are being held, we can carry them away just as they were when they were taken from us."

Jason thought for a minute.

"It may work. But how will you get close enough?"

"I suggest that Eled and I steal the uniforms of two sentries – there will only be two, I'm sure. They will be complacent as they think that you humans are beneath them and that you pose little threat. The next part of the plan is the part that I do not like, and you will hate. We will take one of the nurses with us, as an act of deception to make them think that we have captured another female to sell."

Jason shook his head.

"You're right. I don't like it. It's too much to ask someone to do. We could end up with three women being sold into slavery."

Siroll nodded.

"I know it is horrible. But it is our best chance. We do not know how much time we have. And Enak and Eled will not let any harm come to the nurse."

Jason still wasn't sure.

"Will they be safe overnight?"

Siroll nodded. "They will not be treated

particularly well, but they will be safe. Their captors will not wish to damage their merchandise. They are safe for tonight, anyway."

Jason reluctantly agreed to the plan.

"Where do you think they're being kept?"

Enak pointed at a ten-storey building nearby. Jason scrambled over to one of the Marines.

"Marine Geek. What's that building over there?"

"The hotel? That's the Key Bridge Marriott Hotel."

"Do you know anything about it?"

"I know some."

"Tell the Argons anything you know."

Jason then moved across to where the two nurses were reminiscing about safer times.

"Hi girls. Sorry to interrupt, but Enak has a plan to rescue Sitara and Miriam. The only problem is that we need your help. And it'll be dangerous."

Both women, US Marine Corps Nurses, were eager to help, but the rescue mission only needed one of them. For a few seconds, there was a little light relief as the choice was made by the result of a best-of-three battle of rock-paper-scissors. Jason returned to Siroll.

"Roberta has volunteered to help with the rescue. Will the girls be safe during the night?"

"Yes. As I said, they will not want to damage the merchandise. They will be kept in a room inside a charged plasma containment bubble."

"What's that? Some kind of force field?"

"Probably. I do not know what you would call it."

"How can Enak and Eled get the girls out, if they're trapped by force fields?'

"Do you remember the implement I used to repair the damaged arm of Eled?"

"Yes?"

"The tool is very versatile. Mine is out of energy now, but both Eled and Enak still have theirs. They can use them to break the force field."

Now he knew more details, it sounded a very good plan to Jason. It had to be – it was the only plan they had.

"OK. Let's do it. First thing tomorrow morning, as long as the girls will be safe for tonight. Today's been hard. It'll be better for all concerned if we start afresh tomorrow. We'll sleep hidden from view under one of the bridge's arches tonight."

In a room in the Key Bridge Marriot Hotel, Sitara and Miriam were comfortable on the large double bed in a King's Guest Room. As holding cells go it was luxurious and even had a great view. The door wasn't even locked, as Sitara soon discovered when she went to leave and bounced back off an invisible wall. Miriam sighed.

"Why does it always happen to me? I'm sick of being carried off by aliens. I mean, who was nearly carried off during that awful battle? Me. I'm a fucking Argon magnet."

Sitara was shocked to hear an Amish woman swear. She looked at her cell-mate.

"Did...did you just swear?"

Miriam blushed.

"Sorry, Sitara. I didn't mean to. It just slipped out."

"No need to apologise. I was just surprised, that's all."

Miriam grinned.

"I do feel better for cussing though."

Sitara laughed.

"I bet you fucking do."

The two of them burst out laughing.

"I didn't know Muslim women swore, either."

Sitara's eyes glinted.

"Well, I'm not your regular Muslim girl either. Thoroughly modern Muslim, that's me."

Having composed herself, Miriam tried to keep a straight face, but a fit of the giggles overcame her. She fought to control her breathing again.

"Well fuck me."

By now the two girls were in hysterics, both having completely blown away their respective faith's stereotype. A banging on the wall from an adjoining room brought them back to their senses. It was followed by a male voice.

"Is someone there?"

The women weren't sure what to do, shushing each other.

"Please answer. These alien guys don't appear to be able to speak English."

Miriam nudged Sitara.

"Do you think we should?"

Sitara nodded.

"We've nothing to lose."

She went up to the wall and spoke in a voice loud enough for their fellow prisoner to hear, but not so loud that it might attract unwanted attention.

"Hi. My name is Sitara Khan and my friend is Miriam. Who are you?"

The voice sounded audibly pleased.

"Sitara Khan? It's Roger Nelson."

"Roger Nelson? Administrator Nelson?"

Miriam tugged at Sitara's sleeve.

"Who is he? Do you know him?"

Sitara quickly turned to her friend.

"It's my boss, Miriam. My big, big boss. Administrator Nelson is the boss of NASA."

The voice sounded sad.

"I'm not boss of anything now, NASA's gone. The UN is gone. The whole infrastructure has gone. So many people dead. So many dead, Doctor Khan."

Sitara had mixed emotions. She was happy that Administrator Nelson had survived, but had suddenly been reminded of the millions that were not. She forced the thoughts from her mind. She had bigger fish to fry.

"How did you get here?"

"I've been surviving on my own and saw a group of people crossing the bridge. I thought maybe I could hook up with them. But I was spotted, caught, and brought here."

Miriam finally opened up.

"That was us. We were heading –"

Sitara pressed two fingers to Miriam's lips.

"Shhh. We don't know if they have those translating things. They may be listening."

The fingers removed, Miriam whispered a thank you. Sitara turned her attention back to the wall.

"We'll find a way out of here or get rescued. I'm sure we will. And we'll take you with us, Administrator Nelson."

"Call me Roger, please."

"Only if you call me Sitara, Roger. Now, I think we should probably get some sleep. We don't know what time we'll be rescued."

Miriam's face brightened up.

"You're sure the others will rescue us?"

Sitara lied.

"Of course,"

There was a hope, but it was a slim one; the rest of the group didn't even know that they were still alive.

DAY NINETEEN – 12 MAY

Enak, Eled, and Roberta, the Marine Corps Nurse, woke up just before dawn. The plan was to find an Argon sentry patrol, overpower them, and take their uniforms. Then they would head for the hotel with Roberta as their prisoner, another piece of merchandise for the upcoming auction.

Jason and Samuel watched as the three rescuers turned into silhouettes in the half-light, and headed in the direction of the hotel. Samuel was nervous.

"Do you think they'll get them back, Jason?"

Jason wasn't sure of anything, but couldn't show his own doubts about not only the rescue mission but about whether they were doing the right thing by going to 1812 North Moore. The rest of the group might think that he knew what he was doing but he was just winging it, improvising as he went along. However, the others looked to him for guidance, for leadership, and he couldn't let them down. Without hope, what else did they have? Without hope, what was the point of going on?

"I'm sure they will, Samuel. They know what they're doing."

The rescue party had only walked about two hundred yards from the bridge, and were under the George Washington Memorial Parkway when Eled spotted a two-man Argon patrol approaching them. He pulled the others into the shadows and whispered urgently.

"Two warriors approaching from the left. This is our chance."

Enak reminded the nurse what would happen from thereon.

"Roberta, we will change clothes with these two and then Eled will carry you under his arm while we take you to the hotel. Apologies in advance for any discomfort. From this point, we will speak Argon only. Do not worry, just follow our lead. Are you prepared for this?"

Roberta nodded.

The warriors were almost upon them now. Enak and Eled let them pass and then, without a murmur, each one grabbed a warrior's neck, putting their victims in choke holds before pushing the warriors' heads sharply forwards before jerking them rapidly backwards, breaking the Argons' necks and ripping their windpipes apart for good measure. Roberta was shocked at the ease with which the two Argons were able to kill the sentries – she knew that the Argons were strong, but no human could have done that so efficiently and with so little effort. Enak and Eled quickly swapped clothes with the warriors and Eled checked that Roberta was ready before scooping her up under his arm.

As they passed the low hedge in front of the large black sign that proclaimed the building as the Key Bridge Marriott hotel, a warrior approached them. He gestured at the helpless Roberta, who had obviously given up struggling and resigned herself to her fate.

"*Atapemu enigniwm?*"

Enak grinned.

"*Oyidn. Iznizu enigniwm aw umadanib awk adanm. Akatmanuipaw?*"

The warrior looked Roberta over more closely.

"*Akewmuk ajomap an enignew, akitak abmuhc ahc imuk an enn. Anizal ilabukin, azewukis aununmuk eweynewm – eyey aituvuh onogn, kwa umadanawm.*"

Enak joined in the banter.

"*Adnepegnin aununumuk amak awukilin an asep. Imim teb eyey in abmotuk awbuk.*"

The three Argons laughed heartily and the rescuers continued into the hotel foyer, thankful that Roberta hadn't understood a word that they had said. It hadn't been complimentary. They ignored the other six Argons in the foyer, focusing only on getting to the tenth floor. Fortunately, there was an elevator already waiting and they ducked inside. Enak counted the buttons and decided – correctly – which button served the tenth floor. Their universal translators were great for translating speech, but he had no idea what the strange marks meant when human words were written down.

Upon reaching the tenth floor, the elevator doors opened out onto a corridor. Should they go right or left? Which way led to room 1014? A warrior was standing in the hallway. He couldn't have been there by accident. They approached the warrior and Enak gave the traditional greeting gesture, the palm of the right hand placed over the heart. The guard reciprocated. Enak pointed at Roberta.

"*Atun enigniwm awk ilija uney. Aodno abmahs al uvugn.*"

The Argon did as he was bid and deactivated the force field, before meeting the same fate as the two sentries who had provided the rescuers' uniforms. Recognising Enak and Eled, Miriam almost shrieked her excitement out loud but was stopped by Sitara's hand covering her mouth. The two Argons reconnected their translator devices. Eled gestured that they should follow them, as Sitara whispered to Enak.

"There's a friend of mine in the room next door. We have to take him with us."

"We need the guard's *obmohc*. His *obmohc* activated the force field, only his *obmohc* can deactivate it."

Roberta, grateful to be back on her feet again, picked up an object that had fallen alongside the dead Argon.

"Is this what you're looking for?"

Eled took it from her, thanking her, and deactivated the force field of room 1015. Roger Nelson was reluctant to come out at first, but when Sitara reassured him that the two Argons were friendly, he left his room. The only problem that remained now was how to escape the building. They hadn't properly thought that through beforehand. They couldn't bluff their way past the remaining seven Argons, as they had on their way into the building, not with the freed prisoners. Eled went into the Administrator's room and looked out of the window. He beckoned Enak over to join him. He pointed at the swimming pool, whose water had just started to turn a light shade of green, nobody having cleaned it since the plague took hold.

"Do you remember playing *Aput Ototm* as a child? What do you think, Enak?"

Enak looked at the pool, then at the window, and then the pool again.

"It could work."

Sitara joined them at the window.

"If you're thinking what I think you're thinking, it won't work. There's no way that we can jump into the pool. It's too far away."

The two Argons grinned at each other. Enak explained.

"We are not going to jump. Well, you are not. We will throw you into the pool. *Aput Ototm* means throw the child. It is a game we used to play as children, we would throw our smaller friends into a lake, Eled and I can make the jump, but we will throw you."

Sitara looked at the pool again, not sure that she wanted to be thrown out of a window. Eled pointed out the choices.

"It is either that, or you become prisoners again.

The Argons want to sell you as sex slaves."

That made Miriam's mind up.

"Sitara. I am NOT staying here to be someone's sex slave. Guys, I'm ready."

Enak opened the window and carefully removed the frame from its mountings, with as little noise as possible, leaving a large gaping hole in the wall for them to escape through. Miriam smiled at Eled.

"I'm ready."

Eled scooped the young woman into his arms, checked the trajectory, applied a little backspin and launched Miriam into the void. The sensation was exhilarating, what she imagined a theme park ride would be like, but she managed not to scream. Sitara, Roberta, and Roger Nelson landed in the water in quick succession, followed by Enak and Eled, who had expertly placed the humans so that they wouldn't collide with each other in the pool.

The six clambered out of the pool, dripping wet, but safe and unhurt. Enak grinned at his friend.

"The skill never abandons us."

They ran as fast as they could towards the bridge, pausing only to retrieve their clothes from under the Parkway, and turned to watch as the hotel crumbled to the ground. Roger was wide-eyed.

"What the hell did you do?"

"We left an *obmohc* behind and created a reverse polarity gravity charge chain reaction. Basically, we separated the molecules holding the building together."

A few minutes later, they were reunited with the rest of the group, who were still tucked beneath the arch of the Key Bridge. After celebratory hugs and fist bumps were over, it was time to return to the main objective, getting safely to one of the top floors of 1812 North Moore. That was as far as they had planned ahead. Nobody had any idea what they would do next. They didn't know how they were going to defeat the Argons – everything they did now was improvisation – and all they were doing was surviving. Each day that they didn't die was a small victory, but could they win the war that was looming? The Argon's biological pre-emptive strike had been so effective and was going to rid the planet of almost 98 percent of humanity.

The day's objective was still to reach 1812 North Moore. They certainly couldn't stay under the arch, and if they didn't go to the building, what else could they do? The Argons that had died at the Marriott Hotel would be missed. Enak had explained that they were probably a scavenging party from a much larger group and that when they didn't return, there would be more Argons sent out to find out why. And if the humans defeated this next group, then more would come. To make matters worse, the Argon warrior groups that were scattered around the planet weren't even the main invasion force. Millions of Argons could be expected to arrive any day. Even with a very liberal estimate of 160 million human plague survivors, it still wouldn't be enough to defeat the technical and numerical might of the Argon invasion.

Those survivors would also be spread across the planet, many in remote areas, and couldn't possibly be united to defeat the Argons.

Perhaps 1812 North Moore Street wouldn't be the end of homo sapiens' existence on the beautiful planet that they call home, but it could well turn out to be the last stand of Jason's small band of survivors.

After a brief and thankfully uneventful walk from the bridge to 1812 North Moore, the thirteen humans and three Argons arrived at the building and looked up. A Marine took his helmet off and wiped his brow.

"Damn, that's a long way up. What floor are we going to?"

Marine Geek removed his helmet.

"Three hundred and ninety feet, including the antenna spire. Thirty-five floors. I recommend we go to the thirty-third floor; The floor space reduces after that. Plus it's two floors less to walk."

A third Marine didn't like the sound of that.

"You mean you want us to walk up thirty-three floors, Geeky? Fuck that. I'm taking the elevator."

"There was a standby power generation emergency system, an engine-driven 1,250 kW, 480/277V, three-phase generator with automatic controls."

"You said was."

"Yeah. There was. But it would have started up automatically when the main power went down. It had an eight-hour fuel supply. That will have gone now."

Like the rest of the group, Jason was looking up to the top of the building.

"So, what you're saying is that it's Shanks's pony or stay here, Marine Geek;"

"Shanks's what?"

"Shanks's pony. Use your legs. Walk."

"Jeez. You Brits have some crazy sayings."

And so the long trek into the heavens began. Climbing thirty-three floors would have been bad enough if they had been travelling light but, weighed down by rucksacks, it was an arduous task. Jasmine was only six years old and did her best, but an ascent that was proving tough for the adults was almost impossible for her. She managed fourteen flights of stairs before she slumped to the floor, her little legs unable to take the strain for another nineteen flights. John, her father, started to carry her up the staircase along with his own heavily laden backpack, but gratefully accepted Eled's offer of help. The Argon had saved Jasmine's life in the massacre at L'Enfant Plaza and John knew that, much as he wanted to carry his daughter up to the thirty-third floor himself, Eled would hardly notice the additional weight.

By now, it had become second nature for Enak to take the lead and for Jason to follow the group from the rear, but this time the pair reversed positions. Any threat was perceived to come from the rear, and it made sense for the Argon to protect the column. Caution was definitely the better part of valour. It took over forty-five minutes for the whole group to reach the thirty-third floor; the climbers had varying levels of stamina and fitness, and those that found it easier than the others were forced to continually stop and wait for the slower members to catch up. But nobody was irritated by the frequent rest stops – recent experiences had fused the two groups together into a micro-community.

Jason didn't really know what to expect when he opened the door from the stairwell on the thirty-third floor, but it didn't really matter. He knew from checking the list of tenants in the lobby that the floor had been occupied by a large multinational insurance company's sales division, so he wasn't expecting anything other than a commercial environment. The centre of the floor space was taken up by the reception area, the elevator lobby, a file room and two copy workrooms. The rooms that the survivors were most interested in, however, were the lunch room and the restrooms – that was where any comfort lay. An outer ring of thirty-six workstation areas gave way to an outer perimeter of thirty-five small individual offices, broken only by two conference rooms on the eastern side of the building. It would probably have felt more welcoming if it had been a little more open-plan, but at least this way everybody could find some privacy if and when they wanted it.

The rest of the group exited the stairwell and half of them made a bee-line for the restrooms, bladders desperate for relief, before gathering in the reception area to agree on their next move. Once everybody had returned, Jason sat on the reception desk and addressed his small congregation.

"The main reason I wanted us to find a high-altitude refuge was so we could see if any Argons are approaching. It's a centuries-old strategy; the defenders in the old days always looked for a high geographical location, as it's much easier for us to defend a higher position point than for them to attack one. That gives us the advantage."

John, his daughter Jasmine having dozed off on his lap, was understandably worried about the future; he was the only one who, if it came down to the wire, had to think about someone else other than himself.

"How long do you see us staying here, Jason?"

"Maybe two or three days. I don't think it's a good idea for us to get too settled here. I'm thinking of this place as a temporary stepping stone until we decide where to go next. The views will give us a good opportunity to check out which is the safest direction. I don't think it's a good idea to stay in the big city too much longer."

The group seemed okay with that. Enak also had a strange but valid point to make.

"I think that we should be prepared in case we are attacked again before we rest. I suggest that we unplug the electrical equipment."

One of the Marines quipped.

"What are we going to do with them? Throw them at the Argons?"

Enak nodded.

"I sense that you are making a joke, but that is

exactly what we will do. A computer monitor or computer is a primitive weapon, but it may afford you valuable seconds of life."

DAY TWENTY – 13 MAY

The night was peaceful, as was the group of survivors. They hadn't been able to relax for days, and even now the sense of calm that appeared to run through the group was but a mask, hiding the true feelings of trepidation. What did the future hold for them? Could the Argons be defeated? Were they simply postponing the inevitable, trying to eke out the last vestiges of life?

Little Jasmine was the lucky one. She didn't understand the recent events and could only take them at face value – those which her mind allowed her to remember, that is. She'd seen her mother ripped apart in front of her eyes, and had almost been trampled to death before being rescued by Eled. She didn't need to remember those experiences and her young mind had taken a decision to blot out the memory. All that she was fully aware of was that her daddy was with her, and if daddy was there, then everything would be alright. He'd look after her.

Others were not so lucky. Jasmine's father John was wracked with guilt, questioning himself as to whether there was anything he could have done to save his wife, Annette. She had suddenly gone into mother tiger mode, prepared to die in order that her daughter might live. She had put her own body between the Argon and Jasmine and paid for it with her life. To her, it wasn't a choice and nor was it a duty. It was just Nature. Her daughter must survive, no matter the cost. John had had problems of his own, having been thrown against a wall, stunning him momentarily, and had come back to full consciousness to see the final seconds of his beloved Annette's life as her head was ripped from her body. The next thing he remembered was suddenly seeing his daughter flying through the air towards him and his instincts took over as his arms unconsciously moved into position to catch the young child. It was only when he dived into a side room and sat down against a wall, cradling his crying daughter in his arms, that he realized that it was Eled who had thrown her away from certain death.

Samuel and his sister Miriam were struggling with their own forms of guilt. They were suddenly free of their Amish constraints, the invisible ropes that had bound them ever since their return from their respective rumspringa. Samuel had loved the enormous rumspringa parties in the woods that he had attended and was missing the opportunity to drink a beer now and again. He'd got really drunk on a couple of occasions but had certainly not enjoyed the hangover the next day, learning quickly to drink in moderation. He wasn't craving beer, but he did like the taste, and quite fancied a cold beer after climbing all those stairs.

Miriam felt double the guilt of her brother. She hadn't experimented with alcohol or gone to any woodland parties, but she had entered into a sexual relationship with Hannes, a young lad from the Geauga County community of Ohio. Nobody knew about this relationship – not even her brother – and nobody could ever know about it. The couple knew that it was a sin, that their parents would never have accepted the intensity of their relationship, but they couldn't help themselves. They hadn't intended to fall in love, much less to have suddenly found themselves exploring and enjoying each other's bodies, but their emotions and feelings had somehow managed to ride roughshod over their strict Amish upbringing, an invisible mutual connection and desire that couldn't be denied. Although they had both returned home to their individual communities, they'd kept in touch by using fake accounts on Facebook and WhatsApp, using cell phones that were kept hidden well away from prying eyes. They chatted at least twice a week via video call and had even tried having video-sex a couple of times; not a satisfying exercise for either of them.

Miriam had been trying to sum up the courage to tell her parents that she wanted to leave the community and the religion for some time, and now she had been robbed of the chance to be honest with them. She hadn't wanted to hurt them, but she had to think of her own life, her own future. Added to that, she now had no idea if Hannes was dead or if he was still alive. She had no idea what his blood type was; it wasn't the kind of thing that you talked about while making love. She prayed – she still believed in God, even though it wasn't in the way that her parents would have approved of – that Hannes was alive, that his blood group was B Negative. She hadn't even had the chance to fetch the phone from its hiding place before they left the farmstead, not that it would have helped much even if she had it with her. There was no electrical power and, ipso facto, the cell phone networks were down. Plus, the phone battery wouldn't have lasted forever. The group had passed a few shops in their travels where she could have stocked up with spare batteries, enabling her at least to look over past messages and the dozens of photos of the couple that were stored in the phone's memory, but it would also have meant admitting the tryst to her parents and almost certainly led to a full-scale argument – something she wished to avoid. She would have told them about Hannes when the time was right, but the right time had never arrived. Now it never would.

Sitara had abandoned her Ramadan fasting, not through choice but by necessity. It was impractical to not eat during the day – nobody could be sure where the next meal was coming from – and practicality trumped religion in these circumstances. She was certain that Allah would forgive her; he knew what was in her heart and would understand that changes to how she followed her faith had been necessary. A long conversation with Roger Nelson and Jason had diminished but not erased the guilt that she still felt at having been instrumental in the spread of the pandemic. She sometimes wished that the Bering Sea had swallowed her up and taken her down to a watery grave but, obviously, that hadn't been Allah's will. But had it been the will of Allah to sentence ninety-eight percent of the world's population to a torturous death? Surely he couldn't have wished that upon his children. What had they done to deserve that? It was becoming more and more difficult to reconcile the fact that Allah had allowed the Argons to send the plague to destroy humanity so cruelly. Jacob had said that Argons were also Allah's children – had he really chosen them over mankind?

The survivors, those who weren't on lookout duty, slept the broken sleep of those with troubled minds. Occasionally someone would awake with a start, escaping a nightmare. Others would continue sleeping but the twitching of facial expressions betrayed the dark thoughts and memories that were racing through their sub consciences. Mercifully, Jasmine's mind protected her from these nightmares, allowing her the sleep of the innocent.

Jason opened his eyes without warning as a Marine shook him awake. He blinked three times and then saw Marine Geek standing above him.

"Jason. You need to come look at this."

He followed the Marine into a perimeter office that looked out onto North Moore Street and beyond towards downtown Washington DC. The Marine pointed out of the window, handing his binoculars to the Brit.

"Look towards the Key Bridge."

Jason did as he was told and almost physically felt his chin drop. Up to one hundred Argon warriors were gathered on the DC side of the bridge, preparing to cross from Georgetown to Arlington.

"Shit!"

The Marine pointed downwards.

"And look down there."

A lone figure had just emerged from Gateway Park, part running, part staggering. Jason focused the binoculars on the figure, thankful that they were top-grade high-powered military issue. He took the binoculars away from his eyes before returning to look at the obviously frightened man. He'd seen the man before and audibly showed his surprise.

"I don't fucking believe it."

He handed the binoculars back to Marine Geek before leaving the small office and kneeling down alongside Enak. He shook the Argon awake.

"Enak. Enak, wake up. I need to show you something."

Enak stood up and followed Jason to where the Marine was patiently waiting. The Marine handed the binoculars to him. Jason whispered.

"Look at the Key Bridge. The other side. That's not good."

Enak nodded.

"No, it is not good. News of what happened to the scavenger party has obviously got back to Argon Control."

"Now pan down to the figure that's just come out of the woods."

"Where?"

"The road that we used to come here. The one that passes what used to be the hotel."

"I see him."

"That's not an Argon."

"You are correct in your appraisal. It is a human."

"Take another look. Can you see his face?"

Enak focused the binoculars on the man's face, realising what Jason's next question would be, and understanding the can of worms that was about to be opened.

"I see his face and can identify him. It is the human that calls himself Triggs."

Jason turned around and punched the door, hard enough to express his frustration but not hard enough to wake anyone else up.

"Fuck, fuck, fuck!"

Jason turned back to see the Marine and the Argon waiting for his next move. Marine Geek didn't understand the problem.

"Who's Triggs?"

Jason leaned against the wall of the office.

"We met him – I say met, but really we were attacked by him and his gang – when we spent the night at the Millers' farmstead."

"The Amish family?"

"Yes. The Amish family. Anyway, he and his mates turned up during the night with plans to rob the place and rape the women. Maybe even kill everyone. But they hadn't reckoned on me, Enak, and Sitara being in the barn and stopping them."

"So what do you want to do?"

"I don't know. My instincts tell me he's a no-good son of a bitch, and to just leave him there to his fate, but he's still a human."

Enak looked from the Marine to the ex-paratrooper.

"Indeed you have a problem. Empathy brings problems with it. And it is a problem that must be resolved quickly. The Argon warriors will not stay on the far side of the bridge forever."

Jason pulled his body away from the wall.

"Wait here. I'll be back in a minute."

He disappeared from the room and quickly returned, flanked by Sitara, Samuel, and Miriam. Unsure of how the three newcomers would react to the news, he paced around the small room. He had to say something; he hadn't brought them into the room to admire the view.

"There's someone heading this way. A human."

Miriam didn't think twice.

"Then we must let him in."

Jason pulled his lips tight.

"It's not that simple."

"Why not?"

"He could be working with the Argons. Could he be working with the Argons, Enak?"

The Argon shook his head.

"Argon warriors will see him as beneath them. They have no problem initiating deception, but it would be an affront to their honour, dignity, and courage to rely upon a traitor to beat their enemy."

That was going to make the decision more difficult. Should they abandon the man to his fate, probably sentencing him to being ripped apart, or should they save him, potentially only putting off the same fate by a few hours, maybe only a few minutes? Samuel agreed with his sister.

"If he's not with the Argons, then we have a duty to save him. A human and moral duty. We can't just leave him out there to die."

Jason knew that he had to bring up the elephant in the room, an elephant that only he and Enak knew about.

"You may change your minds in a minute."

Sitara was in agreement with the Amish siblings.

"I agree with Samuel and Miriam. Human life is sacred, especially now. If we can save him, we must. We have to at least try."

Normally Jason would have agreed with them, but – armed with additional knowledge – part of him knew that they couldn't trust the man.

"The man is Triggs."

Sitara was the first to react.

"Triggs? Are you sure?"

"Both Enak and I have identified him. It's Triggs alright."

Marine Geek interrupted them.

"You'll have to make a decision quickly, or it'll be too late either way. He's getting closer."

Samuel held his sister's hand.

"I think Miriam should decide. After all, it was her that they were going to rape."

Miriam glared at her brother.

"How can you leave it all up to me? I'm not going to live – if I carry on living – with that on my conscience alone."

The clock was ticking. A decision had to be made. It sounded callous, but Jason had a way to force a decision, one way or another.

"Rock, paper, scissors?"

Sitara and the Amish turned towards their friend. Sitara couldn't believe her ears.

"Rock, paper, scissors? Are you seriously suggesting we should leave this decision to a game of chance? You'll be suggesting rock, paper, scissors, lizard, Spock next."

Miriam wasn't happy, but someone had to make a decision.

"Bring him in."

Jason was glad someone had bitten the bullet.

"Are you sure?"

"Yes. I'm sure. If nothing else he'll increase our manpower by one."

"OK."

Jason addressed the Marine.

"Who's the fittest of you four, Geeky? I mean, who can get downstairs quickest?"

"That'll be Spinks. He runs up and down skyscrapers for charity."

"Go and fetch him, please."

Marine Geek rushed to the other side of the

building and returned with his colleague. Jason explained what he needed.

"I want you to run downstairs – leave your kit here, but take your weapon – and grab a guy – a human guy – as he arrives at front of the building. Treat him as a prisoner and bring him up here. We're rescuing him, but he may not see it that way. And be careful – he's not a nice bloke."

Marine Spinks was happy to be doing something more active at last.

"I'll go fetch him now. Leave it to me."

Ten minutes later, Marine Spinks watched as Triggs approached the building. The guy was an absolute mess, dishevelled, unshaven, and unmistakably in need of a good meal or two. He'd just passed the door of the building when he felt a rifle barrel being pressed against his back. Ordinarily, he'd have put up some resistance but he was too tired and too demoralized to do anything other than to give in to whoever was behind him. A voice behind him spoke sharply.

"You Triggs?"

"Who's askin'?"

"Marine Jeremy Spinks, 1st Battalion, 10th United States Marine Corps. And you, my friend, are under arrest. What's your name, fella?"

"Daniel Trigger Esquire, at your service. Under arrest? Why? What've I done?"

"Probably plenty. But all I know is that I have orders to take you upstairs."

Triggs couldn't be bothered to resist.

"Well alright then. I have nothing better to do this fine night."

"Put your hands behind your back."

"Now, I'm afraid I can't do you that favour."

"It's not a favour, it's an order."

"Well, I can't follow that order, Marine Spinks, on account of I only got one hand. Indeed, I only have one arm as it happens."

Spinks looked at Triggs's jacket sleeve. His left arm was certainly hanging strangely, and there was no hand visible. Just to be certain, he felt the sleeve. It was indeed empty, making the Marine's handcuffs irrelevant. He prodded his prisoner with his rifle.

"I hope you're feeling fit 'cos we have thirty-three flights of stairs to climb. But I'm sure they'll give you some water when we get to the top."

"No elevator?"

"No power."

As they started to climb the stairs, Triggs all the time with the rifle pointing at his back, the prisoner weighed up his chances of escape. Maybe he could have overpowered his captor if he'd had two good arms, but with one arm? This was a trained combat Marine walking up the steps behind him. A Marine with a gun.

Approaching the sixteenth floor Spinks allowed Triggs a few minutes rest. The man was clearly not in the best of condition, and he didn't want to kill him unless it was absolutely necessary. Spinks stayed on his feet, covering Triggs with his rifle, while his captive sat down on a step for a couple of minutes. He gestured to Triggs's lifeless sleeve with his rifle.

"So. Your arm. How did you lose it? Or have you always only had one arm?"

"Nope. Was born with two. Always had two. Till a couple of days ago."

"So what happened?"

"Ran into some of them there cavemen. They got the jump on us. Me, my pal, and my boy, Shaun."

Triggs suddenly stopped his story, as he remembered watching his son die before his eyes. He wiped a solitary tear away from his eye with his good hand.

"One of them there Captain Cavemen grabbed hold of my arm and ripped it clean off. I don't know how I managed it, but I ran as fast as I could, only lookin' back once to see the guy standing there lookin' my severed arm up an' down. Looked like he was fixin' to eat it."

"But you survived."

"Clearly did. I ran an' ran until I felt I'd given them the slip. Then I made me a fire and cauter-, cauter-"

"Cauterized."

"That's the word. I cauterized it. Did a mighty fine job too. Still smells a bit of burning flesh though. You can smell the stump if you like."

The Marine refused the kind offer and the two carried on climbing the staircase.

Eventually, they arrived at the thirty-third floor and Spinks pushed his captive through the exit door and to the right towards the entrance lobby. Everybody was awake and waiting to see who the Marine had brought back with him. Triggs shuffled forward, recognising some faces.

"Well, well, well. If it ain't the Brit, Captain Caveman, them two Amish kids, and the Indian lady. Where're your folks, Amish kids?"

Samuel felt the hackles go up on his spine.

"They're dead."

Triggs actually seemed sorry to hear the news.

"Well, I'm saddened to hear that news. I really mean that. Me and my guys had no intention of killing anyone. We just wanted a little fun. Y'know, a little bit of fun."

Miriam gritted her teeth. Maybe she should have left him to die. Jason stepped forward.

"The only reason you're here is to add to our numbers if we have to fight."

Triggs moved his shoulder to allow his sleeve to flap freely.

"Well, Mister Britboy, I'll do my best but I'm a little bit hindered nowadays."

Miriam walked up to Triggs and looked him straight in the eyes.

"And if you so much as breathe wrong – I'll fucking kill you myself, you sick motherfucker. You're only here on my fucking say-so. Remember that."

DAY TWENTY-ONE – 14 MAY

A group of Argon warriors approached 1812 North Moore Street under cover of darkness, from the west, from North Fort Meyer Drive. It was only a small group, ten warriors had been deemed sufficient to overcome these human stragglers. They'd swum across the river unseen and made a long detour to avoid detection by their prey.

They all knew of the deaths of their colleagues at the Key Bridge Hotel, and the humans would pay dearly for their fallen comrades, especially the three traitors who had abandoned the cause and sided with the humans. Enak, Eled, and Siroll would be taken back to the main group at the bridge and would suffer ritual live vivisection. A message had to be sent that nobody betrays their Argon roots. The humans had placed various items of furniture on the staircases to slow down the advance of any attack, but they were futile attempts at defence. These warriors were the elite, the Imperial Bodyguard, and negotiated such flimsy obstacles without a sound, checking floor by floor, until they heard voices the other side of the door to floor thirty-three.

The humans were expecting some kind of attack but thought that they would at least have some kind of warning of an impending assault. They'd been watching the Argons gathered at the far side of the bridge and had seen nothing to suggest that an attack was imminent.

Once the Argons burst through the doors, they were met with a barrage of flying computer monitors and desktop PCs, which they swatted away like children swatting away a fly. An almighty roar bellowed from the throats of the attackers as they launched themselves at the humans.

Gunfire filled the room as the defenders tried desperately to see off the Argon assault. The Argon commander barked orders at his men, catching a Marine's neck in a death grip and twisted the soldier's head with the other, the sound of the cracking of his bones interspersed with the rat-a-tat of bullets spewing forth from his falling automatic rifle, and ricocheting around the room for a few seconds.

Marine Geek leapt onto the back of another warrior who was about to issue the same fate to Sitara and, with one clean motion, his bayonet sliced open a gaping hole across the Argon's throat, a wound that caused the man to immediately drop to the floor as his body vomited blood from the Sicilian smile.

Enak pushed his thumbs hard into the eyes of the Argon commander, whom he had wrestled to the floor and pinned in place with his powerful legs. The commander's eyeballs became a white and red syrup, oozing slowly and uncomfortably out of their sockets, dripping down his cheeks, No longer able to see, the Argon was powerless to prevent Enak from smashing his fist into the alien's chest, the shock of the blow stopping his heart immediately. Enak looked over to where Sitara was trying to extricate herself from the dead body of her attacker who had fallen on top of her in his death throes. He ran over to the scientist and lifted the dead Argon off her.

"Are you alright?"

Sitara was far from alright, covered in the Argon's blood, but she was alive. Enak rifled through the dead warrior's utility pockets and pulled out an object, which he passed to Sitara.

"Here take this. It will help you."

Sitara thought she recognised the thing in her hand.

"Is this what I think it is?"

"Yes. It is his *izimutam ahc obmoh*. His molecule manipulator."

Now Sitara understood.

"The bone-breaker?"

"Yes. The bone-breaker. A good name, for that is how you will use it. Position it on the body of your opponent and press the red button. If it does not kill him, it will severely damage him."

"But I thought it was for healing?"

"If you press the blue button, yes. However, if you press the red button it will disperse the molecules."

Enak then turned and launched himself once more into the affray, while Sitara targeted an Argon who had Miriam in his sights. The warrior, blind to everything but his prey, didn't hear the scientist's approach and let out an agonising scream as she forced the weapon against his neck and the bones within rearranged themselves into a disorganised tangle of calcium.

Although without the physical strength of his Argon friends, Jason was holding his own against the Argon invaders. After leaving the British Army he had continued his Kung Fu training and learned to master the Wing Chun one inch punch technique that the late Bruce Lee had popularised. The Argons had never seen anything like it and, although it didn't generate enough force to kill them outright, it was sufficient to knock them off balance for long enough that the ex-Para could pummel their heads in with the stock of his now empty Remington semi-automatic rifle. He instinctively ducked as Daniel Triggs's severed right arm flew towards him, splattering him with blood as it grazed his shoulder. This was shaping up to be a repeat of the metro station massacre, although there would almost certainly be no survivors this time.

And then...silence.

Jason looked around, unable to comprehend what was happening. He looked at Sitara who, in turn, looked at him, her eyes blinking in astonishment. Jason heard a noise behind him and turned to see Enak, just as confused as the two of them. It was as if they were looking at a still photograph, or somebody had hit the pause button on a movie. The room was perfectly still, with both humans and Argon warriors frozen in mid-movement, along with three computer monitors and a paper shredder suspended in mid-air. Enak closed his gaping mouth and whispered.

"Are they dead?"

Sitara shrugged her shoulders.

"I don't know. If they were, I think they'd have fallen to the floor, wouldn't they?"

Jason was just as confused.

"Perhaps we're the ones who are dead."

Sitara patted herself down.

"I don't feel dead. Do you?"

The other two shook their heads. A voice behind them startled them and they span round to see somebody approaching them through the group of statues. The newcomer, dressed in a well-tailored magenta Nehru-style suit, smiled as he drew closer.

"Don't be afraid. Nobody's dead."

Sitara wasn't sure that she agreed with the stranger.

"But they're not moving."

The stranger gave a knowing smile.

"They are perfectly healthy. They are in fact moving quite normally. As are you. However, you and they are passing through space-time at different speeds."

Jason wanted answers.

"Who exactly are you? Did you do this?"

"My name is Dracip. We are the Jah, We are from a place hundreds of interdimensional leaps from here."

Sitara grabbed Jason's arm; she had only recently become used to Enak and his colleagues being aliens. She wasn't really ready to meet any more.

"How can you speak Urdu?"

Enak interrupted.

"He is not speaking Urdu, he is speaking Argon."

Sitara insisted.

"No. She's speaking Urdu."

Jason was really confused now.

"It's English. And she is a he."

Dracip's constant smile never faltered.

"You each hear me speaking your own language, and see me as a slightly distorted image of yourself. To Sitara, I look and sound like a sister might. To Jason and Enak I look and sound like a brother. I have created an appearance that would be agreeable to each of you. Sitara, ever curious, was awash with questions.

"So are you real?"

"In the sense that I am a physical three-dimensional representation of each of your species? Yes, I am real, in your dimension."

"And what have you done to the rest of the group?"

"Nothing has happened to them. They are well, Sitara."

Jason felt a little lost. The only science he had

studied had been at school. Dracip continued.

"Time is relative. Time is only relevant when it has a relationship to something else. To your friends, time is continuing at its normal pace. To you, time is also continuing at its normal pace. However, you see them as moving at such a slow speed that any movement is completely imperceptible. For their part, neither human nor Argon eye can discern any difference from normal."

Jason accepted what it was for what it was. He couldn't be bothered to try wrapping his head around the science.

"So we know your name. What are you doing here?"

"I am here to rectify a mistake. It is our responsibility."

"What mistake?"

"The Argon were never supposed to encounter your species. We removed them from your planet over forty thousand of your years ago. But we underestimated the speed of their technological progress. And yours, also. The unmanned spacecraft that left your solar system encountered an Argon vessel, which then used it as what you would call a Trojan Horse to attack your population."

Jason didn't give the scientists the opportunity to ask, what would be to him, irrelevant questions.

"If you knew about it, then why didn't you stop it from happening? Unless you couldn't."

Dracip momentarily lost his smile.

"We could have, but we didn't notice until it was

too late. We had other matters to attend to which took priority."

"What the hell could take priority over humanity being destroyed?"

"Many things, unfortunately. You're not the only life-forms in the Universe. And not the only life-forms under our stewardship."

"Yeah. Well. We found that out to our cost, didn't we?"

Putting aside his anger at the needless loss of lives, Jason asked the sixty-four thousand dollar question.

"What are you going to do about it? Bringing back all those dead people might be a good start."

The smile returned to Dracip's face.

"I'm sorry, but we can't do that. We're not gods, even though you humans have been worshipping us for thousands of years. The resemblance between the words Jah and Jehovah is no coincidence. What we can do, however, is to remove the Argons from your planet and return them to Argon."

Sitara frowned.

"So you're not gods?"

"No. We are not gods. Gods do not exist. You worship your creator –"

"And that's not you?"

"No. We didn't create you. You and I were all created by the same process, a physical event that defies the laws of physics as you understand them. I believe you call it the Big Bang. Those of you not constrained by an insistence upon superstitious anthropomorphism are not entirely correct in your suppositions, but you are close. The rest of you worship a historical event that took place nearly 14 billion of your years ago. It would be quite quaint, had you not used this religious fervour to oppress and kill others that didn't agree with you. A historical event cannot love you. It does not have emotions. It is gone. It has passed. Embrace the future instead."

Jason was more concerned about the immediate danger from the Argons.

"But what good will removing the Argons do? They're so technologically advanced. They'll just come back."

"We will prevent them from leaving Argon for the foreseeable future."

Dracip walked over to the giant plate glass window and indicated that Jason, Sitara, and Enak should follow him. The Argons who were camped on the other side of the river were frozen in time, just like their friends. The Jah went to wave his hand but was stopped by an urgent question from Sitara.

"What will happen to Enak? And Siroll and Eled?"

"They will return to their home planet with the others."

Sitara looked at her Argon friend.

"What will happen to you on Argon, Enak?"

"We have betrayed our Argon heritage. We will be tortured and executed as traitors."

That settled it for Sitara.

"Dracip. I want Enak and his friends to stay here. They'll be killed if they go home."

Enak touched her arm.

"It is okay, Sitara. We knew the risks when we made the decision to turn against our people, to let you humans know what was happening. I only wish we could have prevented it."

Jason looked at Sitara, who nodded. They both knew what the other was thinking. Sitara went to clasp Dracip's hands in hers, but they passed through the alien as if she had been trying to grasp a shadow. She stepped back, surprised.

"Oh. I wasn't expecting that."

The Jah laughed.

"I am both here and not here. I am conversing with millions of other survivors simultaneously."

This was too much for even her brain to deal with, so she didn't even bother to try. She felt a little awkward and let her hands hang by her sides.

"Dracip. We have something on this planet called asylum. If Enak and his friends return to Argon, they will almost certainly die. We can't let them be killed for helping us. We would like to offer asylum to Enak and any other Argon who has helped mankind."

Dracip smiled again.

"It's most irregular, but I will put your suggestion to the other survivors with whom I am conversing."

Five seconds later, Dracip had a response.

"I have spoken to the others, explained your suggestion to them, and the majority agree. It appears that your positive experience with Argons has been frequently replicated. Please look out of the window."

The two humans and Enak suddenly found themselves transported from the main floor area to one of the side offices, watching as the scores of Argon warriors who had been on the other side of Key Bridge simply melted away before their eyes.

Enak, who had been quiet for the most part, ashamed of what his people had done, found his voice.

"Are they back on Argon now?"

"Yes, Enak. They have been returned home, where they will be imprisoned until such time as they can prove to us, beyond a shadow of a doubt, that they will treat other species with respect and compassion. This will probably take hundreds, perhaps thousands, of years to achieve, if indeed it can be achieved at all. They will need to change their culture completely and see empathy as a virtue, not something to be scorned."

The Jah turned away from the window.

"I will say one final thing. Let this be a lesson to you. Your species will, no doubt, recover. Eventually, you will reach for the stars again. Treat any other beings that you may encounter with respect and compassion. If you do not, you too will share the fate of the Argons. We will not make the same mistake again."

A Marine rushed into the room, as the Jah disappeared before their very eyes.

"Jason. They've vanished!"

"Who's vanished?"

"The Argons. They were attacking us and then they weren't. They vanished right in front of our eyes."

The ordeal over, perhaps now was the time to say something profound and inspiring to the group, but Jason was just grateful that he'd managed to survive the last three weeks or so relatively unscathed. He'd leave the clichéd speeches to others if they felt an urge to make them. Instead, he walked back into the reception area, sank into a sofa and closed his eyes – for the first time in what seemed like an age, not fearing what he might see when he opened them again.

ABOUT THE AUTHOR

Greg Krojac was born in 1957 and grew up in Maidenhead, Berkshire. He is the author of six published novels: the *Recarn Chronicles* trilogy (comprising of *Revelation*, *Revolution*, and *Resolution*), *Reality Sandwich*, *The Schrödinger Enigma*, and *The Girl With Acrylic Eyes*.

He currently lives just outside the city of Salvador da Bahia, Brazil.

www.gregkrojac.com

BY THE SAME AUTHOR

REVELATION

PART 1 of THE RECARN CHRONICLES TRILOGY

Thomas McCall wants power – absolute power. The Illuminati gives him that opportunity and when he attains the position of Pindar, the head of the Illuminati, he is determined to keep it forever.

Everybody reincarnates, but only Thomas and his fellow Recarns remember their past lives. If only there were a way to defeat the randomness of reincarnation, and guide released souls to a body of one's choosing, thus negating the inevitability and inconvenience of mortality.

Thomas's dream becomes humanity's worst nightmare as the ruthless leader of the New World Order sets about achieving his goal of eternal global dominion.

REVOLUTION

PART 2 of THE RECARN CHRONICLES TRILOGY

To Caitlin, her lover Marcus appears to be a caring and sensitive man, successful in the City in a near-future world where the New World Order has been established. To those who know him better, he is the man who runs the Illuminati with a brutal and ruthless iron fist. And Caitlin's naivity costs her dear,

Marcus is now forced to fight for his survival on two fronts – the first against One Life, the resistance movement, which has been a constant thorn in his side, and the other against Nathan, the usurped head of the Illuminati, who wants to regain his power.

Can Marcus survive against two foes?

RESOLUTION

PART 3 of THE RECARN CHRONICLES TRILOGY

A massacre at a children's birthday party confirms the worst fears of One Life, the resistance movement; the Recarn problem still exists. A final solution must be found, and the World's population must be freed from Illuminati rule.

But nothing comes without a price, and in this instance, the price is humanity - in more than one sense of the word. The solution is deadly and definitely final.

Is this the end for humankind?

REALITY SANDWICH

Jerome lives alone. All the survivors live alone and isolated, never seeing another human being in the flesh – not since the catastrophic event that left the world outside an uninhabitable wilderness. Only killer cockroaches live outside and acid rain melts anyone who dares to venture out of their apartment.

The survivors are used to this life – it's all they've ever known.

But a noise in Jerome's kitchen is about to turn his world upside down, and everything he knows to be true will be rocked by a reality he never knew existed.

THE GIRL WITH ACRYLIC EYES

The dawn of the 22nd century has given us flying cars, personal comms devices connected directly to our brains, and androids – hundreds of thousands of them. There are cleaner-bots, security-bots, and – of course – sexbots.

And then there's Coppélia.

Coppélia's an android too, but she's unlike any other.

How is she different? Why was she created? Is she a threat? The answer is out of this world.

Printed in Great Britain
by Amazon